Siren Spell

A DragonEye, PI Story

Karina Fabian

LASER COW PRESS

Laser Cow Press

MERRITT ISLAND, FL

Laser Cow Press
Merritt Island, FL
https://fabianspace.com

Publisher's Note: This is a work of fiction. Names, characters, places, and incidents are a product of the author's imagination. Locales and public names are sometimes used for atmospheric purposes. Any resemblance to actual people, living or dead, or to businesses, companies, events, institutions, or locales is completely coincidental.

Cover art by Karina Fabian
DragonEye Logo by Len Fabian

Book Layout © 2017 BookDesignTemplates.com

Siren Spell/Karina Fabian -- 1st ed.
Print ISBN 978-1-956489-10-1

Dedication

To Sarah Crickard, with thanks for all your help coming up with a real mystery to go with Vern's other problems. And also—*memento mori*.

Humaning is hard! You people have my respect. Sort of.

Contents

Author's note: Sometimes, you'll see Vern say, "I and so-and-so," rather than "So-and-so and I." Dragons come first. The exception is, of course, Sister Grace.

Chapter One:
Sausage Dreams and
Stranger Things

One thing about Faerie is that they seem to naturally drift toward the cliché. From interspecies romance (a la *Little Mermaid*) to the prince rescuing the fair maiden, there's not a case where I don't run up against at least one element that's been done to death in fairy tales. It's kind of annoying, really.

But not nearly as annoying as when I'm the one forced to live out the cliché.

It started with a nightmare. How cliché is that? Night terror was probably more accurate. I was in the middle of a burning building, fighting—I didn't know what, but it was dark and nebulous, and my every bite and slash met oily vapor. Yet it was solid enough when it attacked me. It pushed and pummeled me, then pulled and stretched. It kept trying to stuff me into a sinewy bag. Again and again, I'd almost manage to escape, just to get snatched up and stuffed in again. Through a night that felt like days, I felt my teeth get dull, my claws shrink to nubs, my scales grow soft. When the dreams finally faded, it was only because my dream-self had fallen into exhausted stupor.

I woke up to Sister Grace's scream.

I got up fast—or at least I thought I did. Everything felt off, my balance, the room. Even Grace. Colors seemed oddly flat yet too vibrant. I blinked and shook my head.

One thing that was not flat was Grace's expression, a combination of fear and fury. She held her hands out, one as if to cast a spell and one as if to block the sight of me. She angled her head away from me as if keeping me in her sights while trying to not look at me. Was I glowing? Was that why everything looked so wrong to my eyes?

"Who are you and what have you done with Vern?" she demanded.

"What? I'm–" My voice sounded weird. Sounded...

I looked down, saw pale, fleshy, *human* skin.

I screamed. "What happened to me?"

"Tell me what you did to Vern!"

"My scales! What happened to my scales?" I dug my nails into my palms. They were so thin and wimpy. "AAAARGH! My beautiful claws! Where are they?"

"What are you talking about? Who are you?" Grace demanded. "How did you get in here? Where are your clothes?"

I only understood about half of what she said. Panic gripped me. I'd lost my wings! "My tail!" I twisted around.

"Stop that!" Grace shouted, her voice shrill.

Her words hardly registered. My tail was missing! I spun in a circle as if I could catch it.

Grace shrieked again then sang a few notes. I barely took in something fluttering from her room before her comforter accosted me and wrapped itself tightly around me. I tried to slash at it with my useless nails and tear at it with my teeth. My chin got in the way and all I managed to do was snag the fabric. The comforter, however, tightened until the only movement it allowed was my chest expanding as I heaved in great breaths. I tried to move, anyway, and lost my balance. The comforter folded, and I fell on my—tailless!—rump in a sitting position.

"Grace!" I cried. It sounded weird and whiny to my ears. "What's happening?"

"It's Sister Grace," my best friend corrected sternly. "Who are you?"

"It's me! Vern! Someone turned me human!"

It took a while to convince Grace that I was who I said I was, after which, we both panicked again. But eventually, she loosened the blanket enough that I could make my unsteady way to the kitchen. Who knew two legs would be harder to coordinate than four? Grace slid an arm around me to assist me with my balance and guided me into a chair. She was warm and steady and smelled nice to my human nose. Did other humans smell that good?

It was a weird thing to focus on, admittedly, but it did help me calm down.

"I'll make you some tea," she said briskly, "then I'm calling Father Rich."

"What? Why?" I asked as the blanket rearranged itself so I could use my arms. I didn't want anyone to see me like this. It was embarrassing enough that I was seeing myself.

"You're going to need some clothes until we figure this out. I'm not going to be able to examine you for spellwork while you're wearing an enchanted bedspread," she replied. Her voice was sharp, and she set the kettle on the stove with more force than needed.

Well, I was annoyed, too. "It's not my fault dragons don't wear pajamas."

She leaned against the stove and sighed. "You're right. I'm sorry. But something got through our shields to do this, and I don't know how that could have happened. I also don't know how I can counter this spell or how long it will take or even if—"

"Don't say 'if'!"

"If I can't, we'll call in help," she reassured me. "It will be alright, Vern. I promise. I'm going to call Father now. Stay calm."

I promised, but I couldn't help feeling her admonition was more for herself than me.

The tea was Natura's special relaxation blend—minus the CBD, but it did the trick. A mix of chamomile and lavender and other spices, it smelled even better than it tasted. I spent more time breathing in the aroma than sipping. Dragons had excellent senses of smell, but there was something different in the quality of human smelling. It was almost a whole-body experience.

After Grace refilled my cup, I leaned over the cup and breathed in the steam. "Does this smell as good as I think it does?"

Grace chuckled softly as she sipped her own tea. She was calmer, too. "It does smell lovely."

Someone knocked on the door and we jumped. There was a second knock then: "It's me, Father!"

"Oh, thank the saints," Grace said and went to get him. I buried my face in the comforting aroma of my tea and braced myself for my friend's reaction.

Maybe Grace coached him because when he entered the kitchen and I turned around, his reaction was only a double-take and a question: "Are you alright?"

"Do I look alright?" I countered, then reined in my temper. I knew what he had meant. "I'm not in pain or anything. I'm just..."

"Human," Father completed, and swore softly.

"Yeah."

He let out a long breath between pursed lips, then held out the paper bags he was holding. "Well, first thing's first. I brought a variety of warm clothes and shoes. Sister Grace had to guess at the sizes, but hopefully something will fit. I also bought new socks and underwear."

Underwear? I shut my eyes. "I hate being human."

Grace tutted comfortingly. "We'll figure this out. In the meantime, ye can't be prancing about in your altogether."

"Oh, my gosh!" Father said, his gaze on Grace. "Did you see him naked?"

She rubbed her brows, hiding her embarrassment in exasperation. "Oh, that I did. Dragons don't wear pajamas, do they? It was bad enough before he started spinning."

"Spinning?"

"My tail was gone!" I exclaimed. "I panicked."

"You were...chasing your tail?"

"You can't chase what's not there," I snapped.

But he was concentrating on Grace. "Are you sure you're okay?" he asked with deep concern.

"Mortified, but yes, thank you."

"Okay, good. Come on, then, Vern. Let's get you decent."

And he had the decency to wait until we were in the other room before he busted out laughing.

I lost my balance trying to put on underwear.

The rest of my clothing adventure, however, went reasonably well. Grace had given Father an accurate description of my height and weight and general form—I guess she saw enough of it—and he made a good estimate of the sizes. I got a little distracted by how soft the T-shirt was. My fingers fumbled over the button fly of the jeans, which caused some rather odd sensations Father told me to ignore. I rejected the itchy wool sweater.

"Why would anyone wear that?" I demanded, scratching at my arm. It no longer touched my skin—why did I still feel it?

"Try this one." He handed me a fisherman's sweater of soft, thick cotton. It settled heavily on my shoulders. I immediately started to feel warmer. What magic was this?

"This is nice!" I enthused. I wanted a dragon-sized one when I returned to my true form.

I did not like the socks and shoes, even if they did make my feet warmer. Father hadn't found any snow boots, and the sneakers he'd brought were too small. I was stuck with thick, heavy hiking boots. I felt like I'd wrapped my feet in heavy weights.

"What if I need my toes?" I complained as I lifted one foot, then the other. Pressure on the top of my foot, constriction on my ankles. I didn't get the appeal.

"For what? Feet are for walking, and on this floor, you'll be in a world of pain and cold if you go barefoot. Alright. Stand up and turn around— and not like you're chasing your tail."

I did as told, slowly because the shoes gripped the floor in a way I didn't expect.

He looked me over critically. He tutted. "The jeans seem a little tight."

"I like it. It's comforting." Having been tightly swaddled had calmed me down. Maybe the jeans would have the same effect.

Father shrugged. "Just go easy on the donuts, or they'll go from comforting to restrictive real fast."

"Look who's talking." When we met, Father had been on a strict diet under the supervision of his sister, Sister Bernadette. Whenever she went on mission, she put me in charge of watchdogging his caloric intake.

"Exactly. Take it from someone who knows."

I thought about it. "Leave the larger pair, then. If I'm stuck being human, I plan on enjoying it."

"Gluttony is as much a sin for a human as it is a dragon," he warned but left the pair folded on the desk. "Ready?"

Walking in shoes was weird.

"You don't have to lift your feet like that. Just walk naturally."

"If I was walking naturally, I'd be on all fours." I retorted.

With a sigh, Father took me to the back room of the warehouse and made me walk from one end to the other until I didn't look like a toddler or topple over. I missed my tail. Finally, he declared me passable, and we headed to the kitchen. Just in time, too. The smells that wafted from the kitchen triggered another sensation, but one I knew right away. I was starving!

"Better?" I asked Grace as I stepped in. I held my arms wide but resisted doing a spin. With my luck, I'd lose my balance and knock over the table. No way was I risking the food piled there.

Grace gave me a quick once over before declaring, "Much. Thank you, Father Rich. And thank you for the groceries. Would you join us for breakfast? I've made enough."

Just like smell, my palate now affected me differently, too. I'd definitely need those other jeans! What was truly new, however, was feeling all the textures of the food. I rolled the scrambled eggs on my tongue to enjoy the sensation on the roof of my mouth.

"Chew your food, Vern," Grace admonished.

"I will," I said, and scrambled eggs fell out of my mouth.

Father spat out his coffee laughing.

Grace tried to look stern, but a moment later, she was also giggling.

Soon I was laughing too. I felt it in my lungs and my jaw. As a dragon, I felt laughter primarily along my neck. My long, sinuous, beautiful neck.

I stopped laughing.

"Vern?" Grace asked, concerned.

I set down my fork and pushed the plate away. Suddenly, I didn't find this fun anymore. Interesting as being human was, I'd feel a lot better if I knew it were temporary. "Could we work on the spell now?"

I hated how small my voice sounded.

Father wiped his face and started to stand. "I'll get out of your way."

"Nae, Father!" Grace said quickly. "I'd appreciate it if you'd stay and pray."

Father held out his hands over us and prayed. It wasn't the first time Grace had asked him to add his priestly blessings to a spell, and he'd gotten rather good at it, smoothly asking God to guide her hands and her magic as well as for us to get to the bottom of whatever this ridiculous situation was. His words were strong and comforting, and when Grace started to sing her spell, their love swaddled me like a spiritual comforter. I closed my eyes and relaxed.

Grace's hands only hovered over me, trying to get a feel for the magic spell around me, but I felt them, nonetheless. The tingle—both sensation and anticipation—was pleasant in a different way than the comfort I felt. I resisted the urge to lean in. I wondered what the human equivalent of cheek crests were and how it would feel if Grace scratched behind them.

I snickered.

"Vern, calm," Grace chided, making it part of the song.

"It tickles."

Father sighed. "Only you."

When I felt her hands over my cheeks, I opened my eyes.

Oh, wow.

Grace's face was just inches from mine—closer than snout distance, closer than we'd ever been at that angle. She stared at me with that expression of unfocused concentration she got when she was deep into a spell. I knew that look, but I'd never realized how beautiful it was. Of course, usually she had that look because she was healing me from some catastrophic injury, or I was busy guarding her back. Today, it seemed to cast a different spell on me. I scanned her face intently, trying to take in every detail. I wanted to remember this when I became dragon again.

Had I ever noticed how green her eyes were? Of course, I must have—I'm a dragon and a detective. I notice details by nature and by trade. Yet there was something different about the quality of the color. I felt like in the past, my dragon sight picked up something different that never let me see the richness of them like I did now.

The same with her skin. I don't think I ever appreciated the light dusting of freckles on her nose. I now understood why some humans thought they were cute. They added interest to her nose and the curve of her cheeks. She sang in tones rather than words. I could just make out the line of her teeth. I rubbed my tongue over the bottom of my top teeth to see if mine were as flat as hers. Flat and dull. Little nubs of canines. No wonder humans cooked their food.

Still exploring the strangeness of my human teeth with my human tongue, I returned my attention back to her. Were her lips as soft as they looked?

The spell ended then and with it, her unfocused concentration. She met my gaze.

She backed away fast.

"Grace?" Father asked.

When she spoke, it was three little words that too often changed lives.

"This is bad."

"Bad?" I said. My body went cold as all other thoughts fled, and I fell upon that word with dreadful focus. My voice rose and cracked. "What do you mean, 'bad'? What kind of 'bad'? 'Bad' as in..." I could not say, *irrevocable*. "What kind of bad?"

"Easy, Vern," Father soothed, but the way Grace paced, clutching her cross and muttering prayers I could not quite make out did not reassure me.

"Grace?" I pleaded.

Maybe my plaintive tone got through to her. She shuddered, took in a long calming breath, released it, and turned toward me. "Whoever did this is skilled and powerful. I couldn't even find a point to start unraveling it."

I slumped over the table and buried my face in my hands. The gesture felt natural even though

I'd never done it before. I leaned further, my fingers raking into my hair.

"We'll figure this out, Vern. I promise. I just need more time."

But something else had grabbed my attention and would not be denied. "I have hair!"

"Yeah, of course," Father said, confusion coming out as annoyance.

I didn't care. I was pulling my hair, letting it move slowly through my fingertips. "But it's so silky!"

"Do you have ADD?" Father asked.

"But feel it!" I said, running my hands though. That felt nice on my scalp, too. "Grace, feel my hair!"

"Vern!" she snapped. "Focus. Do ye want to stay like this?"

"Of course not." But I kept playing with my hair, pulling at individual strands and larger chunks. Was there a section long enough to rub against my lips?

Grace smacked my hand with a plastic spatula.

"Hey!" I protested, then saw her expression. I'd never seen such mix of distress and fear before. Or had I, just not with human eyes?

"Grace, are you okay?" Father asked.

Of course, she wasn't okay. I knew she wasn't okay. By now, magic should be swirling around her, a mage's equivalent of fight or flight.

But I didn't see it.

I didn't see magic at all.

My face grew cold, and my stomach got heavy. The food within it started to roil in protest. It was hard to breathe.

"Vern?" Father asked.

"I'm blind," I managed to gasp out.

"What?" he waved his hand in front of my face.

I brushed it away. "Not like that. I can't see magic."

I looked around the room, at Grace, at my hands. Nothing. That was why color looked so different to me; I no longer took in the thin film of magic that infused everything. I didn't feel it, either, or smell it, or any of the other nebulous ways I'd taken for granted as a dragon.

I was a creature of magic. How could I not be able to sense it? This was worse than when St. George took away my ability to breathe fire.

"I'm going to be sick." I turned in the chair to rush to the sink, but my head felt too light for my body and my already precarious balance couldn't compensate for the room tilting. I clutched the chair tightly.

"Vern," Father chided. "You have to breathe."

Wasn't I breathing? Was that why things were dark and cloudy in my peripheral vision? Maybe I wasn't taking in magic. I stared at the floor, at the boots constricting my useless human feet, at the blue jeans that no longer comforted me. I was weirdly cold in my extremities. I was dizzy. There was magic all around me—there had to be!—and I couldn't feel any of it. Had it abandoned me? Was that part of the spell, too?

"Vern!" Suddenly Grace was crouched in front of me, her hands on my knees.

Grace! How was I going to protect Grace? How would I protect myself? I couldn't sense magic. Would I see demons? Acediadeus still had it out for me. If he found out how vulnerable I was...

"Vern, listen to me. Breathe with me. In...out... It will be alright. We'll figure this out. It's just going to take some time."

She continued to guide me in breathing, speaking gentle reassurances until I didn't have to force myself to slow my breath and my "full vision" returned—paltry as it was. Okay, so I had natural instead of magically generated binocular vision, but how did humans manage to avoid anything coming at them from the side? I shoved the feeling of vulnerability that thought gave me. I *would* get my full 270-degree-vision back. I would get it back. Grace would find a way.

"Better?" she asked.

I nodded. "Thank you."

"Well, you've done it often enough for me."

She smiled. It was a sweet smile, full of love and gratitude for our past, and it made me smile in return. I reached out to take her hand. It seemed a natural gesture.

She shied away.

"Maybe I should take Vern to the church with me?" Father suggested as Grace stood and brushed off her habit.

What good would that do? Grace could hardly cure me if I was miles away. Besides, I was calmer now. I trusted Grace to figure this out. In the meantime, I needed to get myself together. This wasn't the end of the world, after all, but if we didn't do our job, it could be the end of someone else's.

I shook my head and made myself sit upright. "No. We have work to do."

"Uhhh..." Father regarded me dubiously.

I scowled. "I still have my brain. Besides, our case is time-sensitive."

I exchanged a look with Grace, who nodded in agreement. It was more than just time. One of Grace's many-times-great niece had gone missing after taking a job in the Mundane with a cosmetics company. Siobhan Miraculi had come to visit us on her way to Colorado Springs, where she was to start in the marketing department promoting their newest scent, Persuasion. We'd enjoyed a nice lunch together and helped her get her first cell phone before putting her on the bus to Colorado Springs.

Siobhan's best friend in Faerie had come to us two nights ago, desperate, tear-streaked, and terrified that this horrible world would swallow her up like it had her friend. Siobhan had promised to contact her days ago.

The company insisted she never showed up for her first day of work, and she was not answering her phone. I'd found the phone discarded on the side of Highway 50, shattered from being run over, but there was no blood. I'd combed the surrounding area while Grace had questioned the bus company and the driver.

We'd reported her missing to all the proper Mundane authorities, but this was Grace's kin. We weren't going to sit around while they tried to squeeze a search into their busy schedules. Even if I was transformationally impaired.

Besides, I could use a distraction.

Speaking of distractions, my body was sending me new signals, at once odd and familiar.

"I think I need to go to the bathroom," I announced.

Father closed his eyes. I recognized that resigned look—he was offering up his sacrifice for the souls in Purgatory. "Do you need help?"

"Relax. I babysit the Costas. I helped potty train Frankie. I know how this works."

"Praise be to God!"

I rolled my eyes and excused myself.

"Hey!" Father called after me. "Do you need some Cheery Os?"

So it turned out human plumbing—literal and figurative—is not as straightforward as it looks.

I grumbled under my breath about Cheery Os as I washed my hands. I was too annoyed to enjoy the sensation of the soap lather. I spent a lot of time drying my hands. I got water under my scales and claws sometimes, but I don't remember it being as noticeable as moisture between my fingers.

Once I was satisfied, I put away the towel and turned my attention to the man in the mirror.

Whoa. I looked good.

My hair was black, shiny, and cut in long waves that flattered my cheekbones. My brows were broody, though that could have been my mood, and my eyes were caramelly brown— warm and friendly. It was disconcerting to see them both on the front of my face. Dragon eyes were more to the side. Still, they were set nice and even. My skin had a hint of Mediterranean swarthiness, which made sense since my territory in Faerie was the MedSea.

I tried a few versions of The Grin. Not bad. Not bad at all, although I could not achieve the menace that 125 pointy teeth accomplished naturally. Speaking of teeth...

I pulled back my lips. My teeth were indeed flat and stubby, but acceptably white at least.

A good face. One worthy of a dragon. I wondered how the rest of me measured up.

I was about to pull off my sweater when Father banged on the door. "Did you fall in?"

"I'm fine," I called, annoyed. "Just checking my appearance."

"Vanity is one of the seven deadly sins," he reminded me. "Come out. I gotta leave."

"So you agree I'm attractive?" I teased as I exited the bathroom.

He rolled his eyes. "I like you better as a dragon. I'll try to come back tonight with some stuff—pajamas, that kind of thing. I can teach you to shave if it looks like you'll need it."

Oh! Facial hair! "Does it hurt to grow a beard? If I stay human for any amount of time, it might be interesting to grow one." I rubbed my cheeks, but they felt as smooth as they'd looked in the mirror.

Father sighed. "Do me a favor? Try to keep a low profile and go easy on Grace. Give her some space, okay?"

"Why?"

"She's a little more freaked out about this than she's letting on. Listen, if things get uncomfortable, you can come stay with me, okay?"

"I'm not sleeping in the parish garage."

"I have a guest room, remember?" He just managed to not call me an idiot.

"Right. Yeah. Sure." I had no idea why Grace or I would be uncomfortable together. We'd saved each other's lives, seen each other at our best and worst, and been housemates for over a year now. Thanks to me, she was almost off all her psychiatric medications, and thanks to her, I never felt the need to indulge in five or ten gallons of ethanol to escape my Mundane existence for a night. She'd become the best human friend I'd ever had, and that included St. George, who had remained a sometimes advisor and guide even after his death. But I thanked Father Rich and walked him to the door. At least walking was coming more easily now, even if my feet felt constricted in the boots. Then I went to rejoin Grace in the kitchen.

Chapter Two:
Spells and Sensibility

She'd cleaned up breakfast and was sitting at the kitchen table sipping tea and scribbling notes in a notebook. She hummed under her breath. The sounds were just tones with no melody, kind of a magical diagnostic tool, but it didn't matter. I'd always loved her singing.

Dragons sang, with purrs, growls, clicks, the flap of wings, and roar of flames. We produced sounds most mortal ears could not pick up. In Faerie, dragonsong ranked among the top wonders of the world. Still, our long necks did not allow for the clear strong mix of sounds most mortals achieved. A dragon could never sing as Grace does.

But I wondered.

I mimicked three of her notes before laughing with delight. I could sing!

Grace looked up, surprised. "Vern?"

I grinned widely at her. "How good was that? I can sing."

She set down the pen, smiling. "That was good. Try this."

She sang a scale. I repeated it, then the next one she gave me. She laughed, as delighted as I was.

I pulled out a kitchen chair and sat next to her. "I want to learn how to sing. Teach me a song!" Maybe if we did something she loved, we'd both feel less freaked out about human me. "Teach me 'Amazing Grace.'"

"Vern..."

"Please?" I did my best to imitate the look the Costa kids gave their parents when they wanted something. I tried to imagine cuteness and pleading coming from my eyes and pout. I tried not to grin about being able to purse my lips in a pouty way. If it worked, I'd geek out later.

I could not read her emotions the way I had as a dragon, but she seemed to migrate from unsure to stern to charmed. Finally, she threw up her hands. "Alright! Repeat after me."

I knew the words. She led me line by line through the melody, giving me advice as needed.

"Don't force the high note or it will go sharp. Breathe naturally from the diaphragm." She held a fist just below her belly button to demonstrate. "And open your mouth more."

"That saved a wretch like me..."

"Yes!" she cheered. "Very good! You sing the melody, and I'll sing harmony. Don't follow my voice."

It took a couple of tries, with much chiding and giggling when I jumped on her melody line. I almost wished for my dragon capability of selective hearing, but then I would not have heard how good we sounded when I got it right.

"That was fantastic," I said.

She grinned at me with mock sternness. "I'm nae sure. I may have created a monster. You'll be insufferable now."

"No, I won't," I promised, "but maybe if I have to be human for a while, I should join the choir?"

"Oh, that would be keeping a low profile. Or do ye want to tell everyone about your transformation?"

I shrugged. Good as I sounded, I'd probably get asked to do weddings and funerals. "Okay then, but now I can serenade you with your song."

Now, her expression took on true sternness. "Vurnerrah, that song is about God's grace."

I crossed my arms over my chest. (I'd always wanted to do that!) "And you are God's grace in my life. Do not underestimate how important you are to me."

She smiled and her eyes shone with gratitude. For a moment, the joy between us was almost palpable.

Then she cleared her throat and looked away. "So... Siobhan."

"Right." I bit back a sigh. Playtime was over, and so was our comradely warmth. I rose to get some tea to hide my disappointment. "Let's review, in case..." I wasn't sure how to say it.

"In case the curse has affected your memory as well? 'Tis a curse to have a human brain, is it?"

She grinned teasingly, and I felt my optimism return. Maybe we weren't as bad off as Father Rich thought, after all.

"As long as it's not post-George brain. Compared to that, human brain might be an improvement," I said, referring to the fight I'd had with St. George. In addition to taking my size, my fire, my powers, he also blocked a mammoth chunk of my memory. My online ad may say "Wisdom of the Ages, Knowledge of Eternity," but in fact, it was more limited to the past eight centuries since he brought me low.

I sat down with my tea. "Alright. We know the cell phone was a bust."

She snickered. "Literally and figuratively. So was the bus driver. He was not paying attention to his fares."

"Did he notice the guy in a mohawk sitting behind her?" "Mohawk Man" was someone we made up to test how well a witness paid attention to the people around him.

"Oh, aye, though he couldn't remember when he got off the bus. At least he didn't cause any trouble."

I snorted. "Good to hear."

"Yes, imaginary people can be such a handful sometimes."

Frustrated, I ran my fingers through my hair to push it from my face. It seemed a natural gesture, but Grace eyed me a second before standing to pace.

"So, our driver doesn't know if she got off at Cañon City or Pueblo or Colorado Springs," I continued.

"But she never checked into her hotel," Grace said, "and the company has no record of her coming to work."

"That leaves us with the recruiter," I started, then paused. Grace had grabbed her cross and squeezed her eyes shut tight.

"I should have gone with her," she said. "She's—"

"She's a twenty-three-year-old woman who's made her own way since she was sixteen. She's not a frail child that hasn't grown up or needs to hold someone's hand."

But Grace wasn't hearing me. "We should have asked more questions. She has no experience in the Mundane—and we're the professionals."

I couldn't argue that one. "We had no reason to be suspicious. Besides, we did answer a lot of her questions and doled out a lot of advice. We did what we could to prepare her for the Mundane. You even gave her a bespelled Saint Michael medallion."

"For all the good that's done."

"Hey!" I snapped because one thing I did not want to do as a human was deal with self-recriminations. "For all we know that medallion is keeping her alive right now. She's strong; she's faithful; and she's got us. We'll find her. Let's not give up before we've even started."

"You're right," she said, though she didn't sound convinced. She dropped back into the chair across from me, and her shoulders sagged.

I wanted to comfort her. As a dragon, I would not have hesitated to settle my tail on her shoulders or lay my head on her knees. But I didn't know what to do as a human, and the memory of her pulling away from my touch played strong in my mind, as did Father's warning. Why she'd be more freaked out than me, I could not imagine, but we were finally achieving a steady level of comfort together, and I didn't want to jeopardize that.

Instead of reaching out, I kept to business. "She's a smart girl. She'll have been wary of strangers, even if they seemed nice. If she got off the bus early—and wasn't just nabbed at random—then she went with someone she knew and trusted."

"That brings us back to the recruiter," Grace said. "Emmitt..."

"Barnaby. How about you search for him while I call the company? If he's legit, then I can question him. I want to try my phone touchscreen with my fingers." Normally, I needed a rubber nub on my claw or had to depend on voice.

Then a thought struck me, and I felt a surge of panic. "Where is my phone?"

Dragons have a special pouch for carrying items. How did you think we got all that treasure in our caves—U-Haul? Normally, my phone was in that pouch, and I had earbuds. I definitely did not have the pouch anymore—so what had happened to my phone?

Grace looked at my stomach and grimaced. Together, we headed to the pile of cushions that made my bed and dug around. We both sighed with relief when we found it and the earbuds. I had no idea what we would have done if it was still inside me somehow. How would we extract it? Would I need surgery? How would I explain how it got there?

"What if it had been inside me and rang?" I wondered aloud. Grace burst out with a laugh.

"Here." Still chuckling, she held out the phone.

I reached for it and utterly failed to grasp it. I was still used to claws to help me capture things. Instead, it slipped out of my hands and onto the pillows at Grace's feet.

She stepped back. "Try again but grab it more deeply this time. Put more pressure on it but be careful. We've nae tested your strength, and if you have dragon strength in a human body…"

"I don't feel as strong," I said as I crouched down and grabbed the phone. I held it carefully in one hand while I traced my swipe code. It took a couple of tries to get the right pressure.

"Do you want me to call instead?" Grace asked.

"No," I responded, annoyed at her solicitous tone. "I'll get it. I just need practice."

"If you are going to call as yourself, gruff your voice some."

"Like this?" I said, trying to sound like myself without really knowing how I sounded to human ears. For some reason, I felt like I came off as a bad Batman impersonator.

Which I must have, as Grace sighed and went to the office, returning with an alternate phone we used when we didn't want something traced back to us. Then Grace nodded and left me to make the call while she did research on the computer. That was something I had to try out next. I used a virtual keyboard because my claws ruined standard ones. What did a real keyboard feel like on the pads of one's fingers?

I was musing on the thought when the company answered. I followed the phone tree—having to hang up and call back twice when I tapped the wrong number. But I finally got a hold of someone who sent me to HR.

They had no record of an Emmitt Barnaby in Recruiting or anywhere in Fulfill the Wish Cosmetics. Neither did they have an opening in their Marketing Department.

"We are always taking applications, especially from our Faerie brethren," said the perky young woman on the other side of the line. She seemed both knowledgeable and happy to talk to someone who wasn't complaining, so I let her natter on a bit about the company and why it was such a great place to work at. I wasn't sure how much information would be useful, but there was a lot of it. I asked a few questions when she started to slow down, mostly because I was enjoying my first phone call.

Finally, though, I had to thank her for her time.

"You have any more questions, honey, you just call me back," she said and texted me her direct number.

"That went better than expected," I told Grace as I walked into the office. I perched on the edge of the desk. I'd always wanted to do that! "That was fun, too."

"I could tell," she said, glancing at me disapprovingly before focusing back on the computer. "I didnae know you could flirt."

"I don't," I said, suddenly confused and a little flustered. "I wasn't!"

"You have such a lovely voice," she said in a too-good imitation of mine, "and you know so much. I'm so glad it was you who answered the phone."

"I was being friendly!" I protested. "I wanted to keep her talking. Besides...her voice was nice."

Grace held up her hands in surrender. "I'm sure 'Chad' made her very happy."

"Chad" was the alter ego that went with the phone number I'd used. "I'm sure he did," I replied seriously.

For some reason, that made her expression...change, somehow. Something in her eyes as she looked at me. I liked it. It made me feel warm inside.

The moment passed and she took a deep breath as she turned her attention to the screen. "There are seventeen Emmitt Barnabys on Net.Work. Only five live in the United States and none are in the cosmetics industry or HR."

"And outside the US?"

"Australia, Wales, Bangladesh, Hong Kong."

Not much help there. "How about industries related to cosmetics? Didn't Siobhan say something about him knowing a lot about chemistry?"

She scrolled the options, then shook her head. "Maybe it was a fake name?"

I shook my head, not so much in disagreement but because nothing about this felt right. "But why recruit someone out of Faerie for a Mundane cosmetics company—in Marketing, no less?"

"And why Siobhan?" Grace asked. "She was qualified for the job, certainly, but why abduct her? Lovely as she is, there's nothing that stands out about her. Her Magical blood is diluted enough that she can't wield magic. She's an orphan, so no one to contact for ransom. And she said she met Emmitt and got this job at a job fair. He could hardly have made up the ruse after they'd met. She went there herself looking for a job."

"Time to look up the job fair company, then." I shifted to get a better look at the keyboard. My leg slid off the desk and I toppled.

Chapter Three:
How Do You Solve a
Problem Like Vurnerrah?

We looked up the job fair company. DiversiFae Job Fairs specialized in "expanding diversity by uniting Mundane businesses with Faerie employees!" Apparently, that meant something to Mundanes. Faerie businesspeople hired anyone qualified and handy, which usually meant local. For Faerie workers wanting to live in the Mundane, DiversiFae offered job opportunities and help with visas.

Apparently, they didn't just recruit in Faerie, either. Tomorrow, they were hosting a job fair in the Los Lagos fine arts center. Fulfill the Wish Cosmetics was going to be there.

"I should go," I said. After my spill in the crowded office, we'd taken the laptop to the kitchen and were sitting side by side to read the screen together.

Grace eyed me skeptically.

I answered her look. "You could go and ask questions in an official capacity, I suppose, but if FTW Cosmetics is up to no good, they won't tell you anything. Besides, it'd be too easy to recognize you. Meanwhile, I could go apply, ask all kinds of innocent and nosey questions, maybe even suggest Siobhan as a reference, and no one should think twice."

"Maybe," she said, her fingers tapping a random pattern on the mouse. "But you'll need ID."

Fortunately, getting identification in Faerie was much easier than in the Mundane. All you needed was an official form from the Church or the municipality.

"I'm not asking the duke for a fake ID," I told Grace. I'd have to tell him what happened. He'd never stop laughing.

"Bishop Aiden, then, and he may say, 'No,'" Grace warned. "The Church only produces proof of the Sacraments."

I shrugged. "We can change the date on my baptism certificate—or maybe he could baptize this body."

Grace turned in her chair to face me directly. "Vern! You can't be baptized while under this spell. We don't know how that would affect it."

I blanched. "It could make me human permanently?"

"Maybe? After all, the marriage sacrament—"

"I'm not getting married! Who would I possibly marry?" Why would she even think about such a thing? I had no intention of staying human long enough for a date much less a relationship. The very thought made me feel kind of weird and antsy inside.

"My point..." Grace's voice rose above mine. "...is that it's a sacrament which has been known to add permanency to a spell that turns Magicals human."

"I'm not getting married!"

"Yes, I know! But you're not getting re-baptized, either! One per soul—and you have the same soul. Even so...I dinnae know how this spell works, and until I do, we are not taking any chances, especially not so you can go play human in public."

Play? Suddenly, sitting felt too uncomfortable. Adrenalin demanded action. I shoved the chair back with a scraping of wooden feet on the linoleum floor and rose, pacing behind it so that Grace had to twist herself even more to keep eye contact.

"So, no Sacraments at all?" I asked. "Not even Communion?"

I'd taken communion every Mass I'd attended since my Confirmation over eight centuries ago. The thought of not participating disturbed me almost as much as not being able to fly.

Grace looked pained and unsure. "I... I think Communion should be okay? You receive it as a dragon, after all."

"Confession?" Confession, I might be willing to do without. It was hard enough humbling myself to human standards as a dragon. Now, as an actual human, I'd probably rack up a whole new set of sins without even trying. Of course, no Confession, no Communion.

Grace clutched her cross. "Could you please stop pacing? It's hard to think."

I nodded miserably as I parked my butt against a kitchen counter. A part of me geeked out that I could do that. Tails made the pose awkward, let alone the fact that I wasn't bipedal. It was kind of interesting to feel the narrow pressure of the counter.

Grace had shut her eyes and was counting out Hail Marys, her way of regaining her focus. Watching her lips move made mine tingle. I pressed them together, but that only changed the sensation.

Focus, Vern. Sacraments. Dragons. I tore my gaze from her face and turned my thoughts to my past. My kind had been created on the Eighth Day, after God had had a nice rest and was feeling whimsical. We'd been the last species in all of Faerie to fall from grace, and that had happened while I was in a middle of a fight with St. George. Thus, we didn't have our own adaptations of the sacraments like the other Faerie species did, and by the time George had presented me to the pope, the rest of my kind had fled. Pope Pius decided to keep it simple and adopt me into the human ones. Now that I was human, did that give them more impact on my humanity or my dragon-ness?

Finally, Grace spoke. "Alright... I'm afraid because taking the sacraments in human form could reinforce the ties to this mortality. But on the other hand, Confession and Communion are vital for strengthening the integrity of your soul. It's even more complex since you're an immortal species."

This spell could affect my *soul?*

"I'm getting a headache," I complained.

"Me, too." Grace looked fully miserable. Again my instinct to protect her flared.

I gripped the counter. "You know what? That's why Aiden is Bishop. He can discern about these things. Let's tell him what's going on. It can be his headache, too."

Sometimes, I forget Bishop Aiden and Duke Galen are brothers.

"It's not funny," I growled as we watched Aiden's mouth work to contain the laughter threatening to bubble from his throat. The Diocese of Peebles-on-Tweed was one of the few places that had high-speed Interdimensional

Internet. Now, I was regretting teaching our bishop about video calling.

Fortunately, Aiden was more of a diplomat than his brother. He quickly quelled his mirth. "Of course not. My apologies. Have you figured out how this happened?"

"No," Grace and I replied in concert. Even our morose tones harmonized.

Aiden waited.

I spoke into the silence. "Last night, I dreamed I was being made into a sausage, and I woke up like this."

I really should have phrased that differently. Aiden, bishop and shepherd to the most important archdiocese in Faerie, wrestled with Aiden, the boy who put crickets down girls' dresses and got into mischief with his brother, over how hard to laugh. He must have visited the duke recently.

"It's not funny," I snarled.

Aiden finally turned his gaze to the far wall where I knew a crucifix hung, and the kind Bishop won the fight. "You're correct—the situation is serious. But perhaps, you should reconsider how you describe your dream, apt as the current explanation is."

His eyes changed focus to the screen. "Sister Grace, are you alright?"

Why did people keep asking her that? I was the victim here.

After she reassured him, he asked what help she needed.

"I'm not sure. I've not explored the spell very deeply yet. Perhaps..."

I cut in before she could suggest I stay home and play guinea pig. "We were thinking this form might be useful for a case we're working."

"You're thinking!" Grace corrected hotly.

I ignored the interruption. "It gives me a chance to do some undercover work, follow the tracks of our client."

"Siobhan?" Aiden sighed. "Father Bellamier blessed her just before she left. He's beside himself with worry. Do not take offense, Vurnerrah, but are you sure you can handle yourself as a human?"

If anyone else had asked, I'd have protested at their lack of faith in my abilities. "The job fair is tomorrow evening. I have time to practice."

He nodded. "Maybe this is a practical joke, and the spell will wear off by then," Aiden said. He'd know all about practical jokes, being Galen's brother. "In the meantime, the sacraments you received as a dragon should only strengthen you for the trials. I'd encourage frequent confession and daily Mass."

"You're sure?" Grace asked. I didn't like how nervous she sounded. It made me nervous in return.

But Aiden nodded confidently. "He will need the spiritual fortification for the trials ahead, especially if this lasts longer than a day or two. You, as well."

She ducked her eyes. "Of course, Bishop."

My instincts were telling me I was missing an important subtext. "What does that mean?" I demanded, but the bishop was asking Grace what other help she needed.

"I'm nae sure yet. I've only done a cursory examination. This is a deep magic, though. I dinnae believe it's merely a joke. I just don't understand the purpose."

"Then I advise you both to be careful. Tell as few people as possible."

I resisted the urge to reply with a rude *Duh!* "Of course. What's the point of a disguise if you tell people about it? Not to mention—and no offense—this is a huge demotion for me. Kind of embarrassing."

Grace snickered.

Aiden smirked, "And that is the Vern we know and love."

"Which brings up our other reason for calling," I said. "If I'm going to keep my true identity secret, this identity needs some documentation."

Bishop Aiden nodded thoughtfully. "And asking my brother would be problematic. We would not be lying about your receiving the sacraments. I think we can allow a certain...prevarication of the dates. How old would you say you are in this form?"

"Twenty-five."

"Fourteen!" Grace said almost atop me. She took in my annoyed expression, looked over my body, and sighed in resignation. "Twenty-five is fine."

Again, Aiden smirked. "Vern, I suggest you work on your maturity. I expect you to act your age. I'll have a courier with the papers to you in the morning. Sister Grace, you are sure you'll be alright?"

Again with the people being more concerned with her than me. Worse yet, I didn't think it was an expression of their belief in my competence. I watched her carefully as she assured the bishop— again—that she was fine, and we received his benediction.

When the call ended, she pushed her chair away from me but turned to glare at me directly. "Is there something wrong with your eyes, then? You've been staring at me for the last five minutes."

Her sudden anger made me jump. "I..."

She slumped. "I'm sorry." She rubbed her forehead. "That came out wrong. You probably aren't used to human vision. Even the placement of your eyes is so different. I can't even imagine what you must see as a dragon."

"Hey." I leaned forward and patted her knee briefly. "This is not your fault. No defense is perfect against a determined foe."

"I know." She let out a long miserable sigh. She still didn't look at me.

"You'll save me. I have faith in you. Amazing Grace."

"What if I can't turn you back?" she whispered.

"We'll work it out. At least I'm still gorgeous."

My joke fell flat somehow. Before I could apologize—and I didn't even know why I felt the need to apologize—she shot from her chair and told me to wait while she got some items from her workshop.

We spent the rest of the day examining the limits of the spell, and my personal limits as a human. I did have human strength and reflexes. My hearing, while excellent, remained in the human register; ditto, my eyesight. Not being able to see magic gave me the willies.

Even harder to get used to was human binocular vision. As a dragon, my eyes were on the sides of my head. Yes, like most herbivores, but I was an apex predator and a Magical. Magic enhanced my eyesight. That meant I had keen distance and near vision with an amazingly wide peripheral vision. I about jumped out of my skin when Grace approached me from the side as I was putting the kettle on for tea. That's when I discovered my skin did not protect me against heat like my scales did.

Expletives flowed more easily from a human mouth, I discovered.

I felt everything differently, too. My palm stung. Grace distracted me by giving me some cotton balls to touch with my other hand while she applied ointment.

She looked up and laughed. "What are you doing?"

I was brushing the cotton against my forehead. "Different parts of this body feel things differently."

She tilted her head curiously. "Aye, that's normal. It's not the same for dragons?"

"Not to this degree." I closed my eyes and traced the bridge of my nose with the cotton ball, then touched my lips.

"Enough play," Grace chided briskly. "I need that hand a moment."

I bled like a human, too. Needle pricks hurt.

"You'll be fine, you big baby," Grace chided as she put a band-aid on my finger. Focusing on the tests was settling her mood, and the tension between us had again turned to comradery. "It'll be interesting to see what blood type you are."

"D-negative," I quipped. "And I can't wait to be D-positive again."

She snickered. "I'm betting on O-negative. It's the universal donor, and dragon's blood does have healing qualities."

"I could deal with that."

I rubbed the band-aid-enveloped finger with another. If I tried hard enough, I could imagine it was a scale, although a soft, pliable one.

"Don't play with that," she said.

"It feels weird," I replied. I made a fist, feeling my puny, thin nails press into my fragile, thin skin. "How do you stand it?"

She reached over and uncurled my fingers. "With any luck, you won't have to find out. Alright, now, I need to take all this to my workshop."

"What should I do?"

"Prepare for tomorrow? I'm sure there are videos you can watch?"

"On being human?"

"Job fairs and interviews, you silly dragon! That's something neither of us has had to do."

"Right. Yeah. That makes sense."

Now she was the one reassuring me. She squeezed my hand. I liked that she was still holding it. It's the longest we'd had contact since my transformation. "It will work out, Vurnerrah. We'll figure this out."

Before I could reply or even place my other hand over hers, she'd released me and retired to her workshop. I made myself more tea and started searching for tips to help my cover.

I watched videos, then switched to articles. While reading, I put on music and tried to sing along. "Through Millennia" resonated with me. A dragon could love for millennia, if only mortals lasted that long. How many years would I remain in this form? The thought gave me an uneasy pang. But the song was easy to sing while having some interesting beats.

Eventually, my eyes started drooping. This, at least, was a feeling I recognized.

The living area of our lair was really the warehouse portion. Grace's room was a converted second-floor manager's office, with a small shower under the stairs below. We still had walls of boxes and shelves, mainly because as a dragon, I had hoarder tendencies and did not want to remove the illusion of having treasure. We had cleared a spot at the far end where we created a small separate building, like a large shed, but sturdier. It was Grace's workshop. Normally, when she worked there, I was treated to a fabulous light show in the spectrum of magic. Now, everything was dim and gray. I felt sucker-punched.

My nest was not much more than a pile of cushions and old mattresses. It was comfortable and warm...for a dragon. I flopped about, rearranged some things, and pulled out some blankets from Grace's stash. Finally, I laid down and shut my eyes, exhausted.

A few minutes later, I got up again and dug through the bag of clothes Father had brought and found some comfortable sweatpants to sleep in.

Chapter Four:
When Victor Met Gloria

I woke up with a start from a nightmare that immediately fled my memory. I flopped back against the pillows and waited for my breathing to calm. Gradually, I grew aware of a presence above my head. I twisted my neck to look.

Grace was asleep, curled along the edge of the cushions that made my nest.

I had fallen asleep when she was still working in her workshop. I didn't know what time she'd gone to bed, but I must have awakened her with nightmares I no longer remembered, and she'd come down. Her habit tangled around her, but she didn't have her wimple on. Tight red curls shrouded her head like a cloud. They looked fluffy. Were they silky like my hair or soft like a cotton ball?

I wanted to reach out and touch them. My hand itched with the desire. She was asleep. I could reach out, caress her hair gently enough that she'd never know.

What was I thinking? That was my best friend lying above my head. She was curled up like she was trying to stay warm. The only reason for her being down here was because she'd come to comfort me. How many nightmares had I had that she'd decided to stay?

No way would I betray that trust.

Between the aftermath of my dreams and the temptation of her fluffy hair, there was no way I'd get back to sleep. I rose, placed a cover over her, and made my way to the kitchen.

By the time Grace walked into the kitchen, habit and wimple in place, I'd managed to figure out the coffee pot. The stove seemed like too much of a challenge—my hand still ached from yesterday, although the skin looked fine—so I was heating up muffins in the microwave.

"I wanted bacon, but I didn't know how long or what temperature to cook it at," I told her as I handed her a cup of coffee. "Bacon's much easier when I can breathe fire on it."

At 30 seconds, the microwave rang, and I rescued the muffins and set them on a plate in the middle of the table. Then I sat down with my own cup of coffee. I'd tried my first cup with milk and sugar and discovered I didn't like the cloying sweetness. I took this one black.

"How many times did I wake you up last night?"

She sipped before answering. "You don't remember? It's nae problem. I came down twice to comfort you. I guess I fell asleep the second time."

"I appreciate it." I understood now how heart-warmed and embarrassed Grace felt when the night terrors made her cry out and I'd go to comfort her.

Just as I did for her those mornings, she reassured me. "'Tis no easy thing being forced to be something you're not—literally. It was nice to be there for you as you have for me so many times."

We shared a companionable moment, then Grace reached for a muffin. Then another. And a third. Expending magical energy took a lot out of her.

"How late were you up last night?" I was afraid to ask the question I really wanted to know.

She answered it, anyway. "This spell is layered and tight. Someone spent a lot of time and energy creating it. I can sense traps and dodges... I'm afraid to let someone else play with it. I need more time to study it before I can even start to unravel it."

Unravel. That was not a good word in spellcasting. Unraveling spells took time—sometimes years—and had to be done carefully and with great deliberation. One wrong move could make things worse than just accepting one's fate. What would be worse for me in this case?

I put on what I hoped was a confident expression. "I trust you. I can be a human for a while. Dragons treasure new experiences, after all. It'll be fun."

If I could avoid the nightmares and temptations and things I should not do. If I didn't do anything stupid like touching a hot stove. If I could keep Grace from crying or shying away from me.

Yeah. Fun.

When it came time to leave for Mass, I almost climbed into the back of our hatchback like usual. Grace cleared her throat and opened the passenger side door.

"Right. Sorry."

The car was almost as cold as the outside, and my teeth were chattering by the time the heater started spewing out warm air. I did not understand how my torso would be comfortable while my nose and fingers felt like ice. Dragons kept an even temperature throughout their body—another advantage of being Magical. Grace assured me what I felt was normal and suggested I hold my hands up to the vent until I felt more even.

"Did you not know this?" Grace asked, curiously. "Surely, you've known s'lems to get cold hands and feet."

"S'lem" was the word to describe the mortal races Mundanes might call humanoid: dwarves, elves, trolls, and the like. There's no divine revelation about the order in which each species was brought forth upon the Faerie Earth, so calling them "human-oid" is considered both arrogant and insulting.

"I guess I never thought about it," I said. "I'm sure I noticed, but it never applied to me, after all."

"Rub your hands together. Ye never made a cozy fire to help a poor s'lem ally warm his hands by?" she teased.

I curled my lip at her even as I did as told. "I'd expect them to warm their whole bodies. Hey, that actually does help."

My phone chimed. It was a text from the bishop's office:

Expect a courier to meet you at Daily Mass. Your name is Victor DiGiorgio.

I read it aloud to Grace. "Saint George's Victory? That's not subtle at all."

Grace shrugged. "Victor is a good name. It suits you."

Grace parked in front of the church to let me out, and like a s'lem, I schlepped my way in, shaking off the cold as I entered the blessedly warm church.

Daily Mass never had as big a turnout as Sunday, but when Grace cantored, it always brought in extra people, as well as volunteers. Today was also the high school Mass day. A couple of students were setting up the altar under the direction of their teaching assistant, and the teenage pianist was shaking out his hands. I wondered if his fingers were cold, too. In the pews in front of the choir, a handful of older adults were kneeling and saying a rosary, their quiet prayers a murmuring wave. It was beautiful in a peaceful kind of way, but as a dragon, I'd have been able to tell exactly what they were saying, and who slurred their Ts. I glanced at the crucifix.

I trust You, and I trust Grace, I prayed, *but it'd be nice to know I won't be like this forever. I don't suppose you'd send me a sign?*

"Why are you standing there?" a child's voice asked. "That's weird."

A lot of my life was weird at the moment. I looked down to the angry face of Gloria Costa, Number Six in the Costa clan.

"That's Vern's spot," she said without preamble. "You go there!" She pointed imperiously to the back.

Dragon or not, the next time I babysat, we were going to have a conversation about respecting one's elders. "Where's your mother?"

Just then Mama Bear came running down the aisle. She looked from Gloria to me. "Do we know you?"

She held her daughter by the shoulders, as much to protect her as to hold her back.

"I'm a friend of Vern and Grace—Sister Grace. We're working a case together." I smiled and Rosa smiled back. Her cheeks were pink. Had she just come from outside? I held out my hand. "I'm Victor Di—Ow!

Gloria kicked me in the shin.

"Where's Vern? I want Vern!" Gloria demanded.

"Gloria Rosalita Costa de Gutierrez! You apologize!" Rosa demanded as Gloria declared again that she wanted Vern.

I didn't need dragon hearing to know that conversations were stopping. Even the folks praying the rosary had stammered in their "Our

Father." People were looking at me, including Grace, who from the choir was giving me a look that seemed to say, "This is a low profile, then, is it?"

It was my fault. After the trouble they'd had when Jerry tried to leave the mafia, the Costas had a heightened sense of "stranger danger," and as Vern, I'd done my share to teach them to be assertive about it. I stepped back from my knee-high assailant and gave Rosa a reassuring smile. "It's fine. She's a tough kid. Who am I to compete with a dragon? I'll just go...back there?"

I pointed the direction she had indicated. Gloria scowled at me. She knew when she was being patronized. The Costa children were all too smart by half. That's what I generally loved about them. Now, though, I understood why Rosa sometimes used her slipper as a disciplinary device.

I gimped to the back and slipped into the pew just as the pianist started playing the processional.

As it turned out, Gloria's suggestion, however rudely given, turned out to be a good one. I knew how Mass went, not just for humans but for a variety of species, and I had my own adaptations as a dragon. But everything was different now that *I* was human. Sitting in the back, behind the rosary group and the high school classes, no one saw my lapses.

Naturally, Grace cantoring was always my favorite part, but this time felt different. I could not see the magic swirling about her, but I could sense it in her voice. When she sang, it infused me with joy and a sense of belonging. To be able to add my voice in response—I amended my prayer to ask God to delay any miraculous transformations at least until the Psalm ended.

During the readings and Father's short homily, I found my mind wandering. The stained-glass windows looked different—more vibrant than most colors seemed and without the small flaws in craftsmanship my dragon eyes picked up.

While my eyes didn't see as much, my ears heard more—or rather, I was not able to dismiss the distracting sounds. Shuffling feet, two girls in front of me whispering about a "hottie" and being shushed by their teacher, the road noise outside. As a dragon, I could detect a sound and tune it out. As a human, I had to concentrate on the words coming from the podium—and I found myself distracted by the process itself.

Then came time to kneel. I watched as a gentleman ahead and across the aisle from me pulled down the kneeler and folded his legs, then mimicked his movements. I'd never felt that kind of pressure on my knees. So strange, and yet, as Father raised the Host for all to see and declared it the Body of Christ, it felt right to be in that position: the pressure on my knees, my head bowed over clasped hands. I closed my eyes as the choir sang the communion hymn and someone behind me had to tap my shoulder to let me know it was my turn.

Halfway up the aisle, I glanced toward the choir and caught Grace looking at me. She seemed almost afraid. Could she be right that accepting the sacraments in this form would cement the spell further? But then I was in front of Father, and he was declaring "the Body of Christ" so I said Amen and took the wafer on my tongue. I would trust Father and Bishop Aiden and Christ himself.

The dry wafer melted in my mouth, but I felt a warmth infuse me that had nothing to do with heat. Back in the aisle, I nodded toward Grace before kneeling. It was alright. Better than that, it was right.

Afterward, I knelt in the pew, praying: thanking God for the experience, asking for guidance in finding Siobhan, begging to be changed back soon. I sensed someone slip into the pew in front of me and raised my head from my clasped hands.

Lizzie Santos, the student teacher for the class, grinned at me. I'd known her family since I'd moved across the Gap. Her mother had been a loud protestor of my moving into the parish garage. Lizzie had been afraid of me for years. Now she smiled at me like she wanted to be my best friend. She was pretty, too. I'm sure as a dragon, I'd noticed—I understand aesthetics. But I never realized she was pretty.

"Hi," I managed to say.

"Hi. I'm Elizabeth. Sorry about Baby Gloria earlier. She's a feisty one."

I sat back. "Victor. Feisty is good. Those boots, however, should be registered as weapons."

Elizabeth brought her hands to her mouth and snickered. "Omigosh. You're funny. I've never seen you before. Did I hear you're working with Sister Grace and Vern? Are you their new partner?"

I bullied my brain for a vague but true answer. Her mother was also the parish gossip. And Lizzie's voice was a little too hopeful. She had deep brown eyes.

Low profile, Victor. "We have a common case we're working on. I'm not sure how long I'll be in town."

"Aw. Too bad. Still. You look like a good Catholic. I mean, of course—you're here, right? Anyway, there's a singles group. We meet every third Saturday night after Mass. If you're still around, maybe you'd like to join us?"

Before I could think how to answer, a gruff clearing of the throat saved me. It also gave me a start. I had not seen him approach. This limited peripheral vision was going to take a lot of getting used to.

"Begging your pardon, Missy," said the dwarf priest in the aisle, "but I've some business here with this young man."

"I'll get out of the way then. Listen, grab a bulletin on your way out. The information is in there, along with a contact email. That's me, in case, you know, you want a tour of the town or anything. Have a good day, Father. *Victor*."

She gave him a friendly nod and me a friendlier wink and all but sauntered out.

"Smooth as polished onyx, that one," Father said in dwarvish.

"She used to run across the street anytime she saw me coming," I said back, watching as she dipped her fingers in the font and crossed herself. "She was shy with everyone. She spent last summer as a camp counselor in an English immersion camp in Spain. Really helped with her confidence."

"Aye," he said, but in a way that said he was humoring me at that point. I was not so impaired that I couldn't pick up that tone. "I be Father Stone, by the way—since ye seem too distracted to ask. Father Rich said we should meet in his office."

As we left, I saw Elizabeth in the vestibule with a couple of her female students. She smiled and wagged her fingers at me. I snagged a bulletin and rolled it in my hand and saluted her with it.

"Is that wise?" My companion growled in exasperation as Lizzie and her charges giggled.

"I'm staying in character," I retorted. Besides, it was fun. If I'd tried that move as a dragon, I'd have whacked myself in the snout, and that's not clichéd at all.

I was not moving fast enough for Father. He gave me a little shove toward the offices. I heard a second set of giggles as I went.

Grace was already there with Father Rich. She smiled proudly at me as we entered.

"Vern, you did very well in Mass today, even with Gloria's tantrum."

Father Stone added, "Ach, and he was going right fine for himself afterward, too."

"What?" Grace asked.

"What?" Father echoed.

"What?" I tossed in because I was annoyed and even more confused.

Father Stone regarded me with furrowed brows. "I may be a priest, but I do know what it looks like when a lass is mining for a man."

"What?" the three of us now shouted in concert.

Then Grace and Father Rich both turned on me. "Vern!"

I lifted my hands and shrugged. "I didn't do anything! Lizzie Santos came to talk to me when I was praying and invited me to the singles group. I told her I didn't think I'd be around that long. What was I going to say? I didn't want to be rude."

"Why not?" Father asked. "It's not like you've ever given Elizabeth a second thought. She hasn't gone by 'Lizzie' since she started college two years ago. And you are nothing if not blunt."

I had no good answer. I flopped down into a chair. "Can we get on with discussing my human identity?"

"Fine," Father Stone said and handed me a leather portfolio. "Yer a bastard."

"Hey!" Rich protested.

"In the literal meaning of the word," I said, scanning the documents. "Father unknown, mother died in childbirth. Raised by the Silent Brothers until I left. Good idea."

"We figured the harder it was to ask questions about your past, the easier it would be for you," Father Stone said. "And since you spent the past century with the Silent Brothers, you can talk knowledgeably about them."

"Born on St. George's day, really?" I scowled.

Father Stone shrugged. "Goes with the name. Don't kill the messenger."

I grunted a sigh. St. George was probably laughing it up with all his other saint buddies.

There wasn't a certificate of birth or baptism, but a note saying I had received the sacraments. That was typical when a relative or midwife performed the procedure in an emergency. Such a tragic backstory! Exactly what we needed, though, as it closely matched Siobhan's. The enclosed certificate of confirmation would do for citizenship and help me get my ID in the Mundane. Some letters of recommendation describing my skills and intelligence in very general terms rounded out the package.

"This is good," I declared. "Close enough to Siobhan's that if they are targeting Faerie, I'll fit the type."

I passed the portfolio to Grace, who looked it over with a frown. "I dinnae know if I like the idea of you being a target."

"I can handle myself."

"As a dragon."

"How hard can humaning be? I've watched you lot do it most of your life." It was bravado, and they knew it.

Father Rich coughed, and if in that cough, he said, "Briefs," then I was sure I didn't know what he was talking about. Grace, who had been with me through other Dick van Dyke antics the past day, said nothing. We had to find Siobhan, and she knew she couldn't do it alone.

Father Stone had no opinion. "Alright then, as long as I'm here, let me have a look at this spell."

I endured several minutes of sitting quietly while he examined the magic around me. Grace watched on anxiously. I knew she was thinking about traps, but Father Stone's collar had the red piping of an Inquisitor; he knew how to handle dangerous magic.

Father Stone also got his face up close to mine. He had a very round nose and bushy eyebrows that looked more wiry than soft.

Interesting, but I kept glancing over at Grace who, in addition to needing reassurance, was more pleasant to look at.

Finally, he lowered his hands. "Aye, that's a twisting vein of volatility, that is. I don't like it, not one bit. I think you should come back across the Gap with me."

I sensed as much as saw Grace tense.

I shook my head. "After we find Siobhan and if Grace can't figure it out," I said.

"Well, my job was to give you a new identity, not force you to come with me and get your old one back right away. But don't be too long at it. I feel like there's more danger for you than just the spell. And you, Sister: You'll be alright?"

She nodded.

"Hmph. I'll be praying for the lot of you."

Father invited us for an early lunch and ordered takeout pizza, claiming it was a special occasion—after all, how often did one's dragon friend turn human? I gave him a hard time about keeping his diet, but it was a token effort so I could tell his sister I'd tried. I wanted take-out pizza, too. I loved pizza as a dragon. Would it be better or worse to human taste buds?

"I got soda, too," he said. "I know you don't like the carbonation much as a dragon, but it might be different as a human."

He was right. I loved both pizza and soda!

"Slow down!" Father laughed after I'd wolfed down my fourth slice and followed it up with half a glass of cola. Funny how the sweetness didn't affect me as much as it did with coffee. "Gluttony is one of the seven deadly sins, you know."

"Is the eighth one being a killjoy?" I asked. "I ate this much all the time, and you never chided me then. Besides, who knows how long I'll get to enjoy this?"

"You were four times the weight you are now," Father retorted. "And if you keep that up, you'll be four times the weight again even if you don't become a dragon."

"Be careful indulging yourself," Grace said worriedly. "I'm not sure what hedonism will do to the spell."

"Hedonism?" I laughed.

"Vern..."

"Hedonistic pizza?" I didn't even know why it struck me as funny. Yet it felt so good to laugh so hard. I laughed until my eyes squinted shut and I felt moisture seep out of them. After a moment, Father chuckled, too, though he chided me as well. Grace stayed silent.

A strange sensation in my gut made me pause.

"What's wrong?" Grace asked.

"I'm not sure. I think... I think I'm starting to change!"

"You don't look any different," Father said.

"Inside! I feel different, kind of a rumbling and like something is growing in me wanting to get out."

"Umm... Do you need a bowl?"

"Not that! I'm serious. What if...what if I can breathe fire?"

"You're kidding, right?" But Rich pushed his chair away from me and grabbed a bottle of soda as if to put out whatever I breathed on.

"I don't see any changes in the magic," Grace said.

"But I feel it! It's a burning and—bwaarp!" I belched.

They gaped at me. Then Father smacked the soda bottle on the table so hard it fizzed while he bucked over laughing.

"That's not fair!" I cried. I wasn't sure whether to laugh or cry.

"No more soda for you," Grace chided, taking my glass away while Father slapped the table in mirth.

"Bwaarp," I replied.

Thirty minutes and an antacid later, my stomach was better, but my mood was not.

"It's not fair," I moped on the ride home. "How awesome would it have been to be a human who could breathe fire?"

"You'd destroy your innards, you silly dragon," Grace argued.

"I suppose." I leaned my forehead against the window. It was such an interesting sensation to feel so much difference in temperature even from one part of my face to the other. I found it refreshing, especially since I was suddenly so tired.

I let my eyes droop until we got to the lair.

"I think I know what a 'carb coma' feels like," I said as I dragged my feet up the steps.

"You didn't sleep well last night, either, and you've had a busy morning being human." Grace opened the door and let me in first. She spoke as if to a child, but I was too tired to care.

"It takes a lot out of a drake," I commented. I kicked off my boots with difficulty and set my coat on the hook.

Grace did the same. "Are you sure you want to go to the job fair tonight?"

"It's our only lead. I'll be fine. I've stopped burping."

She sighed. "Alright, then. Why don't you go to my room and take a nap? My bed's more comfortable, and I'll wake you in a couple of hours."

She was right. Her mattress supported me without weird lumps. Plus, it smelled...comforting. I turned on my side, clutched a pillow, and knew nothing until she knocked on the door to wake me.

Chapter Five:
A Model Human

Grace dropped me off in an alley a block away from the arts center, and I walked the rest of the way. The wind had picked up, promising snow— the sleety pelty kind, not the nice puffy flakes. Would I be able to see the individual designs like I could as a dragon? I'd have to find out another day. By the time I'd hurried into the warmth of the building, I was wishing I could breathe fire, burned-out innards or no. Fortunately, I stood in line between two centaurs. Their body heat warmed me up fast.

They had someone taking coats, so I gave up my sheepskin coat and brushed lint off my suit jacket. Father had found me a suit from the ones they collected for the dead whose families couldn't afford one. This one fit a little loose, which went perfectly with my alias of a Faerie immigrant needing a job.

At the check-in station, I gave them my credentials and answered a few questions about Victor's genealogy (mostly "unknown") and work history, and then was directed to help myself to something to drink while I waited with the next group. Remembering my experience at lunch, I chose water and took a seat.

Volunteers moved among the group. One had been cornered by a puca, who engaged them in a lively conversation about what to expect in the fair, how the Faerie population was treated, his personal experiences working with the applicants... I hid my smile behind the materials I'd been given about the employers. Meanwhile, I listened closely for any secrets the puca might elicit from his unwary victim. I noticed others leaning in slightly as they did the same. Pucas were natural information gatherers.

A woman in her early seventies with gray hair and a sweet, dried-apple face, sat next to me. "Mister DiGiorgio?"

"Victor." I held out my hand. Might as well start practicing those interview skills now.

Her eyes sparkled as she took my hand. "Mary. I'm so pleased to meet you. Welcome to the Mundane! I have a temporary ID for you. This will get you started in this world. However, if you get a job with one of the companies here, they'll help you with the necessary paperwork and other hoops, as we call them, to get something more permanent."

I stared bemused at the card. I'd been going at this fake ID thing the hard way all along. "Huh. That's amazing."

"Well, we want to make sure you get started on the right foot. They said you brought some resumes? That's wonderful. We made you some business cards based on the information you gave us. That way you can hand them to the employers you meet."

"Okay." Most Mundanes I knew didn't use business cards; they just texted each other the information or shared their Net.Work links. Guess they expected us to be Old School. That was fine since Victor didn't have any accounts yet. If I stuck around in this form, I'd have to build one, but for now, I played dumb and grateful.

She continued, "I know this must be new for you, but we want to give you every chance of success. You just go in there and be yourself. You seem like a good man."

"I'm trying." I also tried not to smile at the irony of that statement.

She patted my knee. "Good luck, dear."

These people really went all out. I'd have felt guilty if a girl's life weren't at stake.

I watched her as she went back to the volunteer table. Then I ducked my head behind my resumes as she was approached by none other than Kitty McGrue, reporter for the Los Lagos Gazette and incessant pain in my tail.

What was she doing here? A job fair was below what her ego would consider a worthy assignment. Either she was being punished by the Editor in Chief, Jonny Redfeathers, or she'd caught whiff of a big story. That was bad for me. McGrue's instincts for sensing trouble were countered by her knack for putting the facts together and coming to the wrong conclusions. Usually, that meant taking any good and brave deed I'd done and making me look like a menace or worse, incompetent. It was almost Spiderman-level slander, except...

No, no exceptions. She was Jameson to my Spiderman. Hopefully, she'd be just as clueless about Victor as Jameson was about Peter Parker.

I laughed to myself. I read too many comics.

Even so, I was glad when the doors opened, and my group was called while she was still interviewing Mary.

I didn't want to look too focused on Fulfill the Wish Cosmetics, so I started a circuit of the vendor booths first, talking to a few of the others. Grace's worry aside, I seemed to be good at this, making contacts and giving my cards away at the first three booths, who all seemed delighted to talk to me. At the next booth, two of the ladies broke from their conversations to approach me.

Then I became aware of someone watching me from the FTW booth across the aisle. I turned my head. A woman in a silk shirt and black skirt that was way too short for the weather was leaning against the FTW table and staring at me with frank admiration. She crooked her finger at me.

Was it really going to be this easy? I gave the ladies I was talking to my card and made my way to her.

As I got near, I held out my hand. "How do you do? I'm Victor..."

She grabbed my hand by the wrist and pulled me close.

Then she smelled me.

I froze. I've been around humans since the dawn of time, and I hadn't seen that kind of greeting since they'd domesticated the wolves and realized sniffing wasn't all that glamorous a way to get to know someone, after all.

"You smell amazing," she said when she'd backed up to a more respectable distance. "What are you wearing?"

"Clothes?" I had no idea what to reply. My brain had jammed. This was not one of the interview questions I'd prepared for.

Fortunately, she laughed. "Funny! But I meant your cologne. Are you wearing any? What about your soap? Shampoo?"

Well, it was a cosmetics company. I denied the cologne and gave her the names of the cheap soap and toothpaste I'd used. "I didn't have time to shower," I said.

"I'm so glad you didn't," she said. "This raw state shows me exactly what I have to work with. I'm Cassandra, and you want to work for us."

She held out her hand. I knew better than to try the same trick she'd done on me. Besides, she held it between us, palm down, limp-wristed. I'd seen plenty of human courtships. I knew this signal. I took her hand and gallantly bent over it, kissing the fingers lightly. It was hard not to smirk. She was making this all too easy. Still, I liked her straightforward style. Very dragony.

"Victor DiGiorgio," I said as I straightened up, "and why would I want to work for you—or rather, Fulfill the Wish?"

She slipped her arm through mine and led me toward the back of the booth as she started on a canned speech about salary and benefits and "embracing Faerie diversity." She gave my arm a little squeeze when she said "embrace." As Vern, I might have felt bothered by the invasion of personal space by a lesser being, but as Victor, I enjoyed the attention.

She led me past the envious eyes of her coworkers to a small area enclosed with curtains. A greenscreen sheet was draped against the back, and a man sat on a stool fiddling with a camera that had me drooling. Someday, I wanted to be able to afford equipment like that. Incriminating photos were a staple in a PI's job, but all Grace had was an aging Pentax we purchased in a pawn shop.

"Most of all," Cassandra concluded, "you want to work for us because we have the perfect job for you. Donny, darling, I've found him. Meet Victor DiGiorgio."

The photographer looked up from playing with his lens and gasped like it was Christmas. Quickly, he caught himself, clearing his throat and saying more neutrally. "Yes. Yes, I see the potential. I can work with this."

Work with this. Yeah, right. He was drooling over my cheekbones like I was drooling over his camera.

Cassandra turned to me. "How would you like to be the next Fulfill the Wish cover model?"

I busted out laughing. Finally! After years of living among Mundanes, someone was going to pay me for the privilege of sharing my beauty with the world...and I only had to turn human for it to happen.

"You can apply for other positions, too," Cassandra added, mistaking my mirth. "It's just a shame to let all this go to waste." She indicated my human form with a stroke of her hand.

Why not? I had to get into the company somehow, and surely models worked with Marketing. I filled out the application and release form they wanted for my audition photos, making sure it stipulated that they could not use them unless I got the job, or they paid me for them. I'd been learning from my encounters with lawyers, and I was not going to miss an opportunity to make a little side money. Cassandra leaned beside me the whole time, one hand on my shoulder.

All finished with the signing, Cassandra led me back to the green screen. She stepped in close. "May I?"

I shrugged. I had no idea what she was asking, but why not? We were in public. She could hardly knock me out and drag me away.

She loosened my tie and pulled it off, taking her time as it slid through my collar. I could feel the motion along the back of my neck. It gave me a tingly kind of chill. Then she undid the top four buttons of my shirt. The whole time, she looked straight into my eyes. It was a pleasantly uncomfortable experience.

"Better," she said, her voice all business as she brushed imaginary fluff off my lapel. "Now have fun."

"I thought we were." The words escaped my mouth before I knew what I was saying. I didn't even know why I'd said that. But apparently, it was a good call; she winked at me as she took a chair behind the photographer.

Then Donny took over, positioning me in front of the green screen and directing me in how to pose: stand here, put my hand there, lower my chin, tilt my head. Getting a good photo turned out to be more work than I'd expected, but I enjoyed it. It was good training, too. Plus, Cassandra watched the whole time, which gave me a chance to ask questions.

"Aren't the models women?" I asked.

"We use men for the male line of cosmetics," she replied, "or male-female combos."

"Who decides that?"

Donny directed me to look left and smile a little. "Perfect! Oh, god, you're a natural."

Cassandra answered, "Marketing. I'm sure they'll have plenty of work for you."

Bingo! I pounced on that. "So I'll be working with Marketing? Only there's this girl I met in Faerie—Siobhan. She said she might get a job in Marketing and to mention her if I applied."

"Girlfriend?" Something in Cassandra's voice set off alarms. I didn't react but just pulled off my jacket like Donny instructed and tossed it over my shoulder.

"Nah. Not enough time. It was at a pub where I was bumming drinks. All she wanted to do was talk about her job, anyway. Made it sound pretty attractive, working in the Mundane. She told me I should look for Emmitt...Barkley?" I purposely messed up the last name.

Even so, I saw a momentary flash of recognition in her eyes, quickly stifled. "I don't know an Emmitt in the recruiting team. Maybe he's someone they hired extra in Faerie."

"Okay, enough talk!" Donny said irritably. "I need closeups, and expressions are vital. Show me your different smiles."

Ha! Perfect, I'd been labeling my many grins for years. I even practiced them to make sure they had the right effect.

It worked as a human, too. Donny snapped pics and called out praises. "Oh, god, yes. I could do this all day. Now, show me sexy."

I paused, confused. What did dragons know about sexy?

"I'm not sure how?"

Cassandra laughed. "Please, Donny! He hasn't stopped being sexy since he got here."

I hadn't?

Donny pouted. "I mean deliberate. Edgy. Show me...hunger. No, not like pizza hunger. How about smolder?"

I knew how to make things smolder, but my expression? I shrugged.

Cassandra sighed to call attention to herself. She crossed her legs and straightened her skirt. "Try feral."

Feral, I knew! I gave her my feral smile, hoping it translated well with human teeth and forward-facing eyes.

"Oh. My. God," Donny panted. The camera shutter clicked at its fastest speed.

So much for striking fear into the hearts of humans. Somehow, that thought struck me as funny and I laughed.

"Yes! That's good, too. Give me more of that."

Afterward, we crowded around Donny's camera to look at the photos. I whistled. I looked good.

"I'm so glad I talked to you instead of Emmitt," I told Cassandra.

"Who's Emmitt?" Donny asked.

Cassandra shrugged, her shoulder bumping mine. "I have no idea. The only Emmitt I've heard of is in product development. He'd have nothing to do with recruiting. Wrong last name, anyway. His was Smith or Samuels or something like that."

I almost believed her. If I'd not seen that momentary lapse earlier, I would have.

"Maybe I got the name wrong," I said. "Could have sworn it started with an E, though."

She set her head on my shoulder for a quick moment. "Well, don't give it another thought. You're mine, now. And there's one last thing we need to do."

Forty-five minutes later, I met Grace in the alley.

"How did it go?" she asked as I climbed into the passenger seat and put on my seatbelt, inordinately pleased that I remembered to do both. My first real foray into the world as a human had been a rousing success, and my mood was soaring.

I held up my bag for her to see. "Terrific! I got us all kinds of office swag. And there's a water bottle, and some of those little ice packs, and..."

She laughed in a combination of amusement and annoyance. "All well and good, my dragon-in-human-form, but what about Fulfill the Wish Cosmetics?"

"Oh, they gave me shampoo and soap and mousse for my hair—not sure I need it... Ow!" I said when Grace smacked me on the shoulder. "Come on—I haven't even gotten to the best part. Look!"

I held up a gift card and an engraved invitation.

"I've been invited to a party to launch their new Faerie-inspired line of products, and the gift card is so I can go to Raelin's and get some spiffy clothes. If they treated Siobhan half as good as they're treating me, no wonder she was willing to go with them wherever."

Grace looked from the card to my bemused, excited face. Her own expression grew worried.

"What's wrong?"

She put the car in gear and started out the alley. The wipers made a rhythmic thwock-thwock-thwock as they pushed back the snow.

"A party? And they gave you money for an outfit—at Raelin's? That's expensive. Vern, what did you do?"

I preened. "Apparently 'Victor' is male model material."

"I beg your pardon?"

"I spent ten minutes in a back booth posing while Donny the Photographer snapped pics and told me to smile. Did you know for humans, 'feral' and 'sexy' look similar? Here, see for yourself."

I smiled at her like I had at Cassandra for the camera.

She glanced my way, then turned her whole head. I couldn't tell if she was proud or horrified.

The car started to drift off the road.

"Grace!" I yelled.

With a yelp, she regained control of the steering. "What do you think you were doing?" she hollered at me.

"Me? I was just showing you how I smiled. I'm good, right?"

She held the steering wheel in a death grip and stared out the windshield with an intensity better reserved for driving through a blizzard—or trying to not look at the passenger beside her. "This isn't funny, Vurnerrah!"

I slumped back in my seat, pouting. Why was she so angry? I'd thought I'd done a great job. I made contact, got them interested, got some information, even learned a new skill. Plus—swag! "I'm not trying to be funny! I'm trying to be..."

Then it hit me. Smiling sexy at my best friend. Who's a nun. I felt my face heat up in a way that had nothing to do with the warm air coming from the vent. "Oh. Right. Sorry."

"Are ye understanding now?" Her voice was hard and snarky. She still didn't look at me.

"Yes! Sorry! Humaning is hard!"

"Don't ever look at a religious like that again."

"Okay."

"Or anyone under twenty-one." Her hands must have been cramping because she opened and closed them compulsively.

"Alright."

"Or any man."

"The photographer was a man."

Grace was growing more agitated by the minute. "In fact, don't look at anyone like that—not while you're human."

"But what if I get the modeling job?"

"Vern!"

We drove in silence for the next few miles. Silence, except for the thwock of the wipers, the hum of the vent fans. Grace grinding her teeth. Cowed and chagrined, I silently stared at the invite in my hands.

Finally, she asked, "Did you meet Emmitt, then?"

"Interestingly, there is—in theory, because I'm not sure I believe everything Cassandra said—there is no Emmitt in Marketing or HR, but there is one in Product Development. So maybe a chemist or something?"

"Cassandra?"

"The woman who recruited me. Very forward—predatory, even. It was kind of fun, actually."

"I think ye should be wary of such fun," Grace warned, and I could see the tension in her jaw. She was gnashing her teeth again.

However, when it came to the hunt, I had supreme confidence in my abilities. Plus, Grace no longer seemed furious at me. I stretched, a sign of confidence as well as to release the tension knotting my shoulders. "Don't worry. I'm the apex predator. I know how to take care of myself. What was interesting, however, is that FTW made me take a DNA test as part of my initial application."

"That is odd."

"Yeah. She did the swab along my cheek, but it tickled in my jaw. Is that normal? Anyway, she said it was part of their diversity program, but no one else asked about my background, let alone for a DNA sample, and I was offered a couple of jobs on the spot."

"You were?"

"Told you I was good at this." I grinned, but not ferally.

"I still don't like it," Grace said, referring to the situation and not my smile. "They're not just targeting Faerie then, but specific species."

"Sounds like it—if they are responsible for Siobhan's disappearance. We don't have enough evidence to prove that yet," I reminded her.

"I know." She pulled into our parking lot. "Ready?"

We made a dash for the lair. Even so, I was coated in a thin layer of ice by the time we got to the door. Grace's habit had an enchantment that protected it and her from the elements, but even she had to wipe her face when we got in. She spoke a cantrip, and we were dry before I could even complain.

"I'm so glad you're my partner," I said, thinking back to all the times in my life that I'd had to shake sleet off my scales. I had no idea how to do that with hair. I think my human friends just endured sogginess until it dried. We did not have a blow dryer, either.

Grace grunted gruffly and headed to the kitchen. I took the swag bag to the office and then the bathroom, emptying it of the contents as I went. I pulled out the little bottle of sanitizer and sighed. This was the treasure I was reduced to collecting.

I spread a little on my hands. The astringent smell cleared my head. I hadn't even realized the light, happy fog of contentment I'd been operating under. Maybe I owed Grace an apology for being too silly. Silly dragon.

It's because I'm getting my ego stroked, I told myself. *How often does that happen nowadays?* Even if I was in human form, I hadn't been that generally admired in a long time. I had a right to enjoy it, and enjoy it, I did.

Finally, I took the water bottle and the ice packs to the kitchen. Grace had poured us tea.

"I followed up with the authorities while you were out," Grace said as I took a seat opposite her. "Including the morgues. There's no trace of Siobhan."

"Casandra didn't know of a Siobhan being hired either, but she said she only worked this side of the Gap. She'd suggested that Emmitt might be a Faerie they'd hired just for job fairs in Peebles-on-Tweed, but I don't buy it. Still, there are going to be people at the party who are in Marketing, so I'll keep asking."

Grace grimaced. "I'm nae sure I like the idea of you going to this party by yourself."

"I thought of that. Allisandra is doing the catering."

I grinned at Grace, and now, she grinned back. Allisandra owed us a favor after we'd solved the case of the cursed canapés and saved her business from going under.

"You think she'll let me on the waitstaff?"

"Can't hurt to ask. There's no 'Plus One' to this invite, so I'm not sure how else we can worm your way in. Speaking of worms, guess who I saw snooping around. Kitty McGrue."

"At a job fair? Seems a little below her pay grade."

"She was asking questions, but I didn't hear what they were. I figured I'd better give her a wide berth, just in case."

Grace nodded. "We'll see what she's written tomorrow, then."

I thought back. "She didn't have a photographer with her, but I did see her taking photos on her phone. Lots of photos. Want to bet she's doing a puff piece as a cover for something else?"

"Siobhan?"

I shrugged. It was such a weird feeling without wings. "No way to know without asking, and since she hasn't come to us—or more to the point, you—with questions, I'd guess not. After all, we filed the missing persons report."

Grace gazed into her tea, her hands wrapped around the cup, seeking its warmth. I knew the expression on her face. She was worried and bordering on self-blame again.

I reached out and squeezed her arm. "Hey. We'll find her. We just started investigating."

"And our attention is divided between that and..." She opened her hands enough to point in my direction.

I lifted one shoulder. "Eh, let's forget about me for right now. I slip up some, but mostly, I'm humaning just fine. We simply need to use your magic for anything I'm lacking right now. Can we find something of Siobhan's, hair or something, and make a tracking spell?"

"Aye. I could even adapt some of my own blood if necessary. We are kin. You don't think we'll find her at the party, though?"

"No, but if someone at the party has been with her recently...?"

"It might alert the spell! That's brilliant!"

"Don't act so surprised."

She laughed. "Alright. I'll get on it as soon as we've had dinner. In the meantime, aside from swag and a party invitation, what else did you get?"

I held up my phone and opened the texts Donny had sent me. I showed her the first one. "Photos!"

"Oh, Vern!"

Chapter Six:
50 Shades of Drake

I may have been basking in the attention and the tribute yesterday, but I woke up in the morning with a healthy sense of suspicion. I gathered all the nifty little bottles the lovely and possessive Cassandra had bestowed upon me and took them to Grace so she could check them for spells.

"But don't mess up the labels. I need the directions," I warned her. "If they check out, I plan on using them today."

She sighed long-sufferingly but obliged. In the meantime, I called a Rhyde to take me to Raelin's.

Grace dropped me off at a nearby dive that rented by the week, and I waited under the damaged overhang for my ride to show up. I did a double take when a VW Rabbit pulled up and a humanish person with lop ears and a pink, twitchy nose stuck his head out the window. "Victor? Hey! I know you. You were at the job fair, right?"

"You're the puca!" I declared as I got in. "This is a new look." Yesterday, he'd appeared fully human.

"I'm Pyitr, but most people call me Peter. Goes with the face, right? Rabbit reflexes help me drive in this weather. Ears just seem to come with it," he said as we pulled out. "So, going to Raelin's, eh? Pretty swanky, considering where I just picked you up. Guess you got a job?"

"More of an audition, I think," I hedged. "I was invited to the FTW Cosmetics launch party and instructed to upgrade my wardrobe."

"You are living a blessed life, my friend. Have you been in the Mundane long?"

I was not going to start revealing my secrets to a puca. "Some. But if you're a Rhyde driver, why were you at the job fair? Looking for something steadier?"

If he noticed my lobbing the conversation back to him, he didn't mind. "More like exploring my options. I do enjoy being around people, and as a driver, I get to have such wonderful conversations. You know how it is."

For a puca, I did. But I also knew how to play a puca's game. They loved to talk as much as listen, and while they didn't reveal their own secrets, they were known to let others' slip.

"Did you get any interest?"

"Indeed, so. I even had a nice conversation at the FTW booth."

"Hey, maybe we'll work together."

"You'll note I'm not being sent to Raelin's for a new suit." He gave me a rueful grin via the rear-view mirror before taking a left to the downtown area where all the ritzy shops waited in hopes of fleecing tourists or residents with too much money to care.

I made a disappointed sound. "Maybe it depends on the job you're getting. That DNA test was something, wasn't it?"

"The what?"

"They didn't make you take one? Then again, you're full puca, right?"

"Astute you are! But no, no test. To be honest, they didn't seem interested in anyone who didn't have at least some human blood."

As I filed that tidbit away, I snorted and made a derisive comment about "diversity."

"Right you are, my friend."

We pulled up in front of a small shop sandwiched between a bank and a spa. Somehow that seemed oddly appropriate. The only indication it was Raelin's was a small neon R with lots of curlicues and swoops. Pyitr offered to wait while I picked up my outfit. On a whim, I invited him to come in with me.

"No sense running your car heater and wasting gas," I said. Besides, he might pick up some gossip for me to help my case. Plus, if Cassandra was there, I wanted to see her reaction to my new friend.

Unfortunately, my benefactor did not show up, but had apparently called when the shop opened and left instructions. The shopkeeper, who introduced herself as Cher, knew me on sight. She took my gift card—I guess it was more ID than currency—and led me to a dressing room. Three outfits waited on hangers. She looked me over critically and removed one.

She handed me the second. "Try this on for size, and we'll work from there."

Even with the puca's gift for gab, I didn't learn much about the cosmetics company as I tried on one outfit, then another.

"Does everyone get the celebrity treatment?" I asked the shopkeeper who eyed the fit of the pants I was wearing—some Korean style with cuffs above my ankles.

She shook her head. "Definitely not the ChoiHyun. Raymondo, fetch me the LeMonet we just got in? Oh, no, darling; only Cassandra's favorites get this kind of treatment."

Before I could follow up on what that meant, however, Raymondo had draped a pair of pants over my arm and pushed me toward the dressing room. He looked more like a Jorge to me.

"Is that your real name?" I asked and got an extra push in reply.

While I was changing, though, I heard Pyitr and Cher laughing. I felt a pang of uncertainty as I looked at myself in the mirror in my French designer slacks and a buttery gold shirt that made my eyes look even more exotic. It wasn't the outfit. I looked smashing. But I'd done my stint as a pampered pet when St. George reduced me to gecko size and presented me to

Pope Pius. What exactly was the price of being Cassandra's "favorite"?

Did it matter? I was just playing a part for a case. The mission was to find Siobhan—and if I needed to dress pretty and play up to Cassandra's expectations, at least this time, I'd have some fun doing it.

I stepped out and struck one of the poses Donny had taught me.

Cher brought a hand to her heart dramatically, and even Raymondo looked impressed. "This is the one—and it's Cassandra's favorite color. She'll be so pleased."

And just like that, I decided there was only so far I'd go even for a case.

How would Cassandra react to a little rebellion?

A shirt caught my eye—some kind of silk blend, crimson in the sunlight slanting through the window, almost black in the shadows of its folds. It reminded me of my scales. I pointed to it. "Can I try that one on?"

"Great choice," Pyitr said as we climbed back into the car with my new outfit in a long suit bag carefully draped across the back seat. "The gold did look amazing, but the red seems more you. I'm sure Cassandra will love it." He sing-songed the name.

"As long as it gets me the job," I said.

"Oh, I'm sure you'll get the job and a lot more, too," he crooned as we headed back to the lousy side of town. On the way, he explained how Cassandra's "favorites" meant more than just professionally.

Even though I suspected, the confirmation hit hard. I started to say "Fewmets!", thought that might give me away, and quickly changed it to another more human swear word.

"Not that interested, then?" Pyitr said. "Glad I mentioned it. You'll need to tread carefully, my friend. I think she's not the kind to take rejection lightly."

Great. Yet another reason for Grace to worry about me.

For a moment, I toyed with the idea of not telling her. It didn't change my mind about going forward with the charade, and she'd just get upset...

Then I laughed at myself. Just like evil overlords had their own rules that led to their downfall, so did heroes. Withholding potentially vital information from their teammates because it might upset them was top of the list.

"Something is funny?" Pyitr asked.

"Just the irony," I told him and did not explain further. "So what did they say happens to these 'favorites' when Cassandra tires of them?"

"Ah, but that's the mysterious part! Cher says she never sees any of them aside from the one time."

"Wow. She bores that easily? So...did they mention if any ladies got a similar treatment?" Maybe Siobhan had been another of Cassandra's playthings, or Emmitt and Cassandra were closer than she let on and shared the same tailor for their "favorites."

"Oh, you're a bad one to be thinking such things!" Pyitr scolded playfully. "But yes. I wasn't sure how to bring that up to you."

I told him, "Doesn't matter to me. I'm just looking for a job."

We pulled up to my fake flop. I paid the fare and retrieved my stuff. We made arrangements for him to give me a ride to the party later.

"Thanks for the ride and the advice."

I watched until he rounded the corner before going across the street to the coffee shop to wait for Grace. How was I going to explain this to her?

In the end, I decided to lay it all out as matter-of-factly as possible and trust that Sister Grace would act like my business partner and not my best friend.

She came through wonderfully. Take that, cliché!

"These 'favorites,'" she said slowly, tapping one short nail on the table. "Are they all Faerie? Faerie-human hybrids?"

"No one said—at least not that I heard, and I didn't ask Pyitr. He did seem to think I was one of the least star-struck by all the treatment, which implies 'Faerie' to me. Mundanes tend to be more cynical. Still, I'm wondering if we can get ahold of Cassandra's other orders and see if any of them link to missing persons."

"Faerie trafficking?" Grace asked. "But why get people with Magical blood who are nonetheless human?"

"Novelty? A full Magical would be too easy to identify, and they'd die after being away from the Gap for too long."

Magicals like myself depended on the small trickle of ambient magic that flowed from the Gap. Too far away from it, and we grew physically ill. I myself had never traveled farther than Denver, and even then, I had started to feel a slight malaise until I returned home.

Grace, whose grandmother was a siren, had been able to live as far away as Washington, DC, for a few years before the sickness brought her back to Los Lagos and into my life.

Grace seemed to be following my train of thought. "And the lower the percentage of Magical blood, the farther they can go and the longer they'd last. Siobhan could be halfway around the world by now." She shuddered.

"Or it could mean they are still recruiting for their next shipment, and she's being held somewhere nearby," I said. "Or we could be completely off-base, and Cassandra is a red herring. No assumptions."

"Still, I think we should talk to Michael—or at least, I should."

"Agreed." Even in human form, I think my disdain for our current chief of police would show through and I'd give myself away. In return, Captain Michael Santry treated me with a special prejudice he reserved for private investigators and Magical creatures. Sister Grace, meanwhile, had developed a kind of bond with him. He listened to her more readily than me, and in return, she pushed me to work more cooperatively with the local police.

"In the meantime," Grace said, meeting my eyes directly with a stern gaze, "I expect you to be extra careful at this party."

"I think I'll avoid Cassandra as much as possible and if I have to be near her, it will be in a crowd," I promised.

Then a thought struck me. "If this party is legit, that is."

"It is. I called Allisandra, and I'll be part of the catering staff tonight. I'll probably just be refilling the buffet, but if you need me, I'll know."

She passed me a chain with three medallions on it: St. Michael, St. Anthony, and half a mizpah.

"The mizpah will alert me if you are in danger—and vice-versa. The St. Michael is for protection against spells, but I'm not sure how well it will work. It could start attacking the spell you're under right now."

Tentatively, I stretched out my hand toward the medal. A shock of lightning arched from it to my finger, so bright and sudden both Grace and I yelped in surprise. I stuck my finger in my mouth. I didn't know quite why, but sucking on the tip made it feel better. "Okay! No go on Saint Michael until after this case. Then maybe I bury myself under as many as you can create and see if they can blast this out of me."

"Could be uncomfortable," she replied wryly as she pulled it off the chain. "The last one is attuned to Siobhan. If she is anywhere near or if anyone has been with her in the past forty-eight hours or so, it will tingle."

"Good work!"

Finally, she passed back the bottles of FTW product. "Near as I can tell, they are safe. They smell nice, too."

"Excellent. Pyitr is going to meet me at 'my place' at six-thirty."

"And I have to be at Allisandra's at six. Are you okay waiting in the lobby? You might get mugged."

"Let them try. I'm more concerned about ruining my new outfit on their nasty chairs. I can call and tell him to get me at the cafe instead."

Then it seemed like there was nothing more for us to say. After a couple of awkward moments, Grace suggested an early dinner and shooed me out of the kitchen.

"But I want to learn how to cook!" I protested.

"Not today. We do not need you getting your hand burned again or cutting yourself or getting hurt in any way that will hinder your assignment tonight," she said.

I thought it showed a terrible lack of confidence in my abilities, but I schlepped my way to the office to watch some dance videos while she cooked.

Chapter Seven:
Seven Deadly Sins Shoutout:
Pride

"I don't believe this!" I stomped into the kitchen cradling the open laptop in my hands. I set it on the counter. "Look!"

"What?" Grace abandoned the table she was setting and moved behind me to look over my shoulder at the article I'd pulled up. If I hadn't been so annoyed, I would have appreciated how close she stood. My apparent success as Victor the past 24 hours had helped our relationship, it seemed.

I moved the cursor to the caption under the photo of me during my photo shoot, a photo not taken by Donny, but by Kitty McGrue. She'd snapped it from a different booth, catching not just me, but also Cassandra and Donny. I had my jacket crooked in one finger and slung over my back, and I had been laughing. I think that was when Donny had said something about showing more teeth. He hadn't understood what I found so funny about that. Cassandra had come to me to straighten my lapel and chide me, "less laugh, more smile" before standing behind him to draw my attention back to the camera. Kitty caught the scene just as I'd calmed down.

A Faerie candidate mugs it up for the cameras while FTW Cosmetics representatives fill his head with promises of fame and fortune.

Grace grunted. "Seems she doesn't think much of the job fair—or Fulfill the Wish Cosmetics, at least."

"She doesn't think much of me," I corrected. "She thinks I can't do it!"

"Vern..."

"I could definitely be a model and a great one, too. 'Fills his head with promises.' More like directions, and I picked them up fast. Want to see me catwalk?"

Grace stepped back enough to face me fully. "No, I don't want to see you catwalk. What has gotten into you?"

"McGrue! Even when I'm not a dragon, she's finding ways to make me look bad."

"Oh, for pity's sake!" Grace crossed her arms and flung her head so that the fabric of her wimple draped over one shoulder. She brushed it back impatiently. She glared at me but did not explain who she was mad at or why.

I knew why I was mad. "They didn't 'fill my head with fame and fortune.' She wasn't even close enough to hear what they were saying, which, for the record, was mostly stage directions peppered with 'Oh, God!' and 'Yes! Yes!' I am a gorgeous dragon and an even better looking human—if that's possible—and either way, if there's one thing I'm good at, it's display!"

I stepped away from the computer to show off my poses. She turned her back to me and read the article.

"Grace!"

"Yes, yes, you're very pretty," she snapped. Her yeses sounded more testy than admiring. I liked Donny's better. "Did ye even read the article or just skip to the photo of yourself? I think you were right and Kitty's suspicious of FTW for some reason."

I slouched and stuck one hand in my pocket, tilting my head like Donny had shown me. "It's the same-old song. She's suspicious with no idea why. If her 'Kitty senses were tingling' it's probably because she was jealous at how Cassandra was fawning over me."

"Vurnerrah!" Grace picked up the plastic spatula and pointed it at me like a weapon. "You'll save that peacock routine for the party. Now sit down and say an Act of Contrition while I get dinner on."

"Yes, Sister," I murmured like a chagrined schoolboy and sat at the table to do as I was told.

Dinner was light in anticipation of the *hor dourves* at the party, and I forced myself to eat slowly. We dissected the article and found nothing helpful, which we both expected, and then chatted about nothing and anything. She'd called Captain Santry and he said he'd do some checking. I talked about the videos, and she warned me that I should be careful with some of the moves I'd seen, but I retorted that I wasn't planning on breakdancing. The snow was getting worse; she was glad we'd been able to afford new snow tires.

A calm, quiet dinner between friends, but I was glad when it came time for prayers and then getting ready for the party.

I gathered my items to take to the bathroom. "Guess I'll make myself prettier—if that's even possible. I might try singing in the shower, too. Don't humans do that?"

Grace shrugged. "So I've been told. I dinnae know why. I have sung the water warm when the water heater was out. The acoustics are not good."

"I'm going to try, anyway. Might as well get the full human experience." I headed to the bathroom, singing "Amazing Grace." It was such a fun song to sing, I understood now why it was so popular even beyond the religious reasons.

Dragons took showers of a sort. I loved lounging under a roaring waterfall or basking in a warm rain. But I felt the impact of drops with an entire scale, a kind of broad pressure. Now, I felt each individual line of spray separately on my skin. I was enthralled.

I ran my hand, then an entire arm under the spray, marveling. I ducked my head under and laughed in delight as my hair grew heavy with water.

"Showers are awesome!" I shouted to Grace.

"Don't use all the hot water," she shouted back.

Temperatures! I experimented with the faucet, taking it as cold as I could stand, then as hot as I could bear. Finally, I chose an optimal temperature. Try that with a waterfall! I wondered what temperature Grace liked her showers at. Did humans have a common range and was it more or less than 98.6 degrees Fahrenheit?

The soap said, "Shea butter." The lather frothed soft and light, and it was a while before I actually washed just because I enjoyed the thick, silky bubbles on my hands. The shampoo smelled nutty, kind of sweet. I loved how it felt in my hair. Washing my hair was like scratching behind my cheek crests. I wanted to purr. Instead, I started singing.

Grace was right, though. Our bathroom's acoustics were terrible. "Amazing Grace" fell flat and stunted. Our bathroom was not worthy of its magnificence. I tried "Through Millennia." Such a dragony song, although as I sang, I pictured it as a duet, with a person shyly approaching me not for treasure or battle but for the honor of being loved by a dragon and myself magnanimously telling them they already were. Still, even that modern Mundane song did not overcome the nulling properties of our shower.

What about something more folksy? What was that ballad about George's and my battle? Nah, I hated it because it exaggerated the depth of my defeat—humiliating. George had hated it, too, for the same reason. He said it made him look too good. Of course, he'd say that.

How about that song he sang to Beatrice?

Oh, Beatrice, sweet Beatrice
Noble and brave are you
No battle steed can ever compare
To the valor of my dear Bubu

Yeah, it was as cringy as I remembered. Even the patter of the water didn't help.

"You're right, Grace!" I hollered, and when she didn't answer right away, I sang,

Amazing Grace! How right you are
The shower stinks for singing!

I held the high note and tilted my head back. Water sprayed into my nose and down my throat. My song devolved into choking. Enough of that.

I followed the directions for the conditioner, rinsing in cool water.

When I'd finished, I was relaxed and ready to put on my fancy clothes and party like a human. I had this!

My fingers were pruney, and I studied them curiously as I exited the shower. Thus distracted, I stubbed my toe and started to lose my balance. Instinctively, I flared my wings and stretched out my tail to regain it.

I didn't have wings or a tail—just pruney fingers and slippery feet.

I grabbed the shower curtain hoping to break my fall. The tension rod sprang loose and conked me on my perfectly hair-conditioned head as I toppled to the ground.

I did not have this.

"Ow!"

"Vern!" Grace pounded on the door. "Are you alright?"

"Fine," I grumbled as I extricated myself. It's not like she could come in and help me, was it? Once I was free of the plastic curtain, which tried to stick to me, I did a check to be sure I really was okay.

My toe, elbow, and shoulder all hurt, but neither the toe nor elbow looked bruised. Good enough. I tried to look at my shoulder, but no matter how I twisted, I couldn't get a good view. My head refused to turn enough.

I growled with frustration.

Grace must have been loitering by the door because again, she knocked, "What? What's wrong?"

"I can't see my shoulder blade," I complained. "Human necks are so limited!"

"Why...? Never mind, I'm sure they look fine. Get dressed."

I finally managed to twist myself enough to get a glimpse in the mirror. I thought I could see a little discoloration, but between the steam and the bad lighting, I couldn't be sure. Ah, well. It wasn't like I'd be taking my shirt off. If it still hurt later, I'd ask Grace for a healing cantrip.

By the time I got the shower curtain back up, I was mostly dry. The directions on the hair gel said to towel dry, apply sparingly, and style normally. I had no idea what normally meant, so I ran my fingers through my locks and played with them until I liked the result.

The hair on my face had grown thicker and darker over the day. I liked it. It went with the feral smile.

Yeah, I corrected myself. *We're not doing the feral smile, are we, Victor?*

At last, I was ready for the fancy duds. I was getting better at the little buttons, but I hesitated at the top three. For a moment, I remembered Cassandra's hands on my shirt, undoing them, and the warm and pleasant feeling it had given me.

Well, I was playing a role—and it was a party. I left them undone. That, however, presented a new problem. My chain showed. I might get away with the St. Anthony medallion, but the mizpah had a different meaning for Mundanes. I was supposed to be single and free. I considered wrapping the chain around my wrist, but what if I rolled up my sleeves? I tied it around my ankle instead. I wouldn't have a reason to take off my socks, after all.

I stepped out of the bathroom, did a turn for Grace, and paused, smiling—not a feral smile, but my insufferably pleased grin. I already knew the answer, but I asked, anyway. "Am I fetching, or what?"

Silence. Grace stared at me, her mouth working, but no words coming out. She gripped her cross tightly.

"What?" I looked myself over, tried to check my back. Was I bleeding from my shoulders? Were my shoes on the wrong feet?

Finally, she croaked out, "I'm...not sure, not sure you going to this party is such a good idea, after all."

Not again. I crossed my arms and glared at her sternly. If my toe didn't still ache, I might have tapped my foot. "Because...?"

She blushed. "There's...well... Something about this spell I don't understand."

"I feel fine!"

"You're too attractive!" she burst out.

I didn't know whether to be flattered or insulted. "What are you talking about? What is the problem? Dragons are the most magnificent of all God's creations, and I'm one of the most beautiful."

"But you're *not* a dragon right now—not in that form. And... And you're not acting like yourself, either! You're..."

The stammering was getting on my nerves. I'd never heard her stutter like this before. "I'm what?"

"Flirty!"

"I don't even know how to do that!" I protested.

"Exactly! Yet you've been doing it constantly since you changed and with the aptitude of Coyote."

Coyote was a pain-in-the-tail empyre, a Faerie version of a Native American spirit. He had a special skill in charming women that got him out of as much trouble as it got him into. Again, I didn't know whether to be angry or pleased.

"Is that really a bad thing? I'm not taking advantage of anyone."

"You're not? What do you call this outfit?" She both indicated and dismissed my natty clothes with a wave of her hand.

"Cover," I snapped. "I didn't ask for these. They were freely given by someone who admires me. And for that matter, if I'm being uncharacteristically friendly, maybe it's because this is the first time in years—maybe centuries—that I've been treated with the respect and regard I deserve!"

"I do respect you," she yelled.

"You're a minority," I yelled back. "But you know what? I think you're jealous."

"Jealous?" she shrieked then her voice grew dangerous. "Of what, exactly?"

"Of the fact that for the first time, I get to do the fun parts of this job."

"This isn't about fun! It's about Siobhan!"

The acoustics in the lair were awful, too, yet somehow, she'd made her voice echo.

I froze, ashamed.

Time stretched as we stared at each other, both breathing heavily. Who knew arguing took so much lung power?

Under the anger, I saw her fear. She looked so vulnerable all of a sudden. I didn't understand why, but I wanted to protect her as I'd protected her since we became friends. I felt like I should close the distance between us, hug her tightly, maybe let her cry against me. I could actually feel myself doing it, even though I didn't move. But she'd turned her head and wouldn't meet my eyes, and I knew such an offering would not be appreciated. Instead, I broke the silence.

"You're right. I'm sorry. I guess I just got carried away."

She heaved a shaky sigh. "I shouldn't have yelled. I knew people were treating you differently, but I never considered what that would mean to you."

"I'm sorry I accused you of being jealous. I'd say it was childish of me, but..." I shrugged and gave her an ironic, self-deprecating grin.

It had the effect I'd intended. She relaxed and looked at me directly. "...but you've never been a child? Apology accepted. And you are right, as well. You've found some good leads that I could not have, and I can't pursue them like you can."

"So, you're okay with me going to the party?" Not that I was taking "no" for an answer, but I was willing to bargain to make her feel more comfortable.

"As long as you don't get carried away, literally or figuratively."

"I promise I'll be careful."

Things had calmed between us again, and I was almost shivering with relief.

"Speaking of careful," she said, her voice more businesslike now. "There's one more thing I want you to do."

She led me to the kitchen where she'd set out the nail polish. Not just any nail polish, but the special kind that changed color if your drink had been drugged. Grace had modified it to detect spells as well. The clear polish turned red for drugs, blue for magic. She wore it when going undercover—a precaution I'd insisted on and that she now suggested for me. I noticed that her nails were shinier than normal. She'd already done her own.

Still, "Won't people notice?"

She replied with a teasing tone that gave her Irish lilt a little more spark. "You're young, and you're a *model*. No one will think twice."

I could not argue with that logic. I took a seat and held out my hands, fingers splayed.

The polish smelled sharp, but the brush was cool against my nails.

"Don't move," Grace chided as I jerked a little.

"Sorry. It tickles, but it's kind of nice, too."

Grace hummed noncommittally, then shook her head. "I never realized dragons were such... sensualists."

"You were going to say 'hedonist,'" I teased.

I thought about it. Dragons thoroughly enjoyed physical sensations. The heat of our fire as it coursed from our bellies out our mouths. The cool massage of gold coins across our scales as we rolled in our treasures. Flying! I adored my ability to fly. Yet how long had it been since I took time to fully appreciate soaring through the clouds, feeling the mist against the membrane of my wings?

"I've gotten cynical," I said slowly, pondering.

Rather than a sarcastic reply, Grace continued to patiently paint my nails.

"I wish I could blame it on the Great War, or even on George, but I feel like it was creeping up on me even before then. At some point, I'd started taking things for granted."

"Mmm. Maybe there is a bright side to this spell, then?"

"Maybe. I should not take what I've been given for granted, and that includes our friendship."

She smiled, and though she didn't look at me, I saw her eyes sparkle as she applied the last coat of protective paint to my nails.

"All done!" she announced as she screwed on the cap. "You can wait for them to dry, or you can wave your hands around."

"Do you need to ask?" I started flapping my hands and she chuckled.

I realized later that we'd had a mist-in-the-clouds moment.

Chapter Eight:
Partying with Pretty Pam

The Porter mansion was the oldest and largest house in the county, and on the historical registry for the state of Colorado. Nestled in 20 acres of mountain land, it boasted 13 bedrooms, a ballroom, and a magnificent double staircase that was still featured in architectural magazines today. The Victorian-style home had been converted into a convention center and bed-and-breakfast fifteen years ago. Since then, it's hosted five governors, two presidents, a multitude of captains of industry, and the Duke of Peebles-on-Tweed. It's also been the on-location filming site for *Branch Beast 3: Stick it to You.*

...or so I read as I stood on the covered porch while waiting for my group to be admitted.

The doors opened, and twenty of us filed in. We stopped first at a counter where three people took our winter gear and stored it in a back room full of racks. I admired the way they moved from counter to coat rack, almost like a dance. I gave my coat to the clerk who handed me a tag and whisked it away before I'd finished saying thank you. I wandered into the foyer as a woman a couple of people behind me fussed at them about making sure no one messed with her expensive fur.

The placard out front had boasted of the chandelier as well as the staircase, but I didn't have time to admire either before we were hustled into a room across the foyer to watch a presentation. Triple screens blocked the magnificent bookshelves and showed scenes of women succeeding in work, friendships, and romance—all, we were led to believe, thanks to a few puffs of perfume. A British woman intoned over the speakers: *Success. Confidence. Seduction. Have it all with the right Persuasion.*

The commercials ended with a crystal, apple-shaped bottle of pink perfume. No symbolism there.

The scene switched to a lab where a couple of too-attractive scientists (probably actors paying the parts) launched into a generic explanation about how Fulfill the Wish Cosmetics was "combining the best in Mundane and Faerie technology" to develop scents that did what was previously thought impossible.

"Or at least highly improbable," one chiseled-faced scientist joked.

Only a couple of us snickered at the line. I guess we knew who the nerds in the group were.

They followed up with charts of studies demonstrating that women wearing Persuasion indeed felt more confidence, and that was leading to greater success in business, friendships, and romance. The video ended with a male scientist challenging us to discover who was wearing Persuasion at the party.

The lights went up and a guy who could have been an actor stepped to center stage. He wore a suit Cassandra would have approved of. A somewhat more ordinary woman took station a half step behind and to his right. She wore a lab coat that while small, still hung loosely on her. The tight ponytail made her look nerdy and young. All she needed were heavy plastic-framed glasses. She gave the audience a tight smile before turning her attention back to her boss.

Slick introduced himself as Pierce Corman, VP of Marketing, and the young woman as Pam Mercer from Product Development. "Pam is one of our rising stars on our science team. Her job is to verify the integrity of our scientific analysis. We're here to answer your questions."

I perked up. I wondered if she knew Emmitt. My movement caught her attention. She glanced at me quickly and just as quickly looked away. I hadn't even smiled at her.

Definitely not wearing Persuasion, but probably needed to.

I must have gotten in with a group of accountants. I let a few people ask about market shares and production before raising my hand.

"Miz Mercer, what exactly do you mean by 'Faerie technology'? Surely, you're not talking about magic."

VP Stage Hog started to launch into a canned explanation that they weren't using magic, as that would ruin the effectiveness of the product past a certain distance from the Gap. I interrupted him before he could explain that to his clueless audience.

"Yes, true, but I was asking Miz Mercer. What, exactly, is 'Faerie technology'?"

She started nervously, "Well, I mean, any sufficiently analyzed magic is indistinguishable from science."

I busted out laughing. Little One had a sense of humor. Unfortunately, we were the only ones laughing. I turned to glare at the people around me. "Don't any of you read?"

I scoffed at the heathens and gave my attention back to her and my question. "So?" I prompted Petite Pam.

Emboldened by the handsome young model-to-be laughing at her nerdy joke—a.k.a., Yours Truly—she stepped forward. "So, seriously. It's because the Faerie have magic that their approach to science differs so greatly from ours. Their understanding of biochemistry is actually decades ahead of ours, plus it's more... Not natural, but more in tune with reactions that happen organically—not organically in the scientific meaning of the word but—"

"Homeopathy," someone in the back interrupted with a disdainful sniff.

Pam did not retreat into her shell like I had thought she would. "Don't discount homeopathy. Many remedies considered homeopathic today were cutting edge when they were discovered, and many are effective. At any rate, Faerie tech is not homeopathy as we consider it. They put in a lot of study and experimentation, with trials as rigorous as those in any lab in the States. It's just that they have a greater understanding of how organisms work, and a wider variety of intelligent, sapient species to develop their own practices."

Color me impressed. Someone thought the Faerie scientists were more than hedge witches. "So how many Faerie scientists do you have on staff?" I asked.

She hesitated. "Oh! Um... I don't really know. Most are still in our labs in Faerie. I'm sure we could get some numbers for you if you're writing an article?" She looked at the V.P. who nodded.

But I just waved my hand dismissively. "Just curious." So maybe Emmitt was in a Faerie lab? That would explain why the Colorado Springs HR department didn't recognize his name. But why not kidnap Siobhan there, then?

VP Spotlight guided back Pam with an open palm as he said something political about learning from their Faerie compatriots, then launched into an inspirational speech about the future of cosmetics as a way to improve self-esteem and not just by looking good. Then they released us to the party.

Everyone else bustled through the rotunda, their minds on free drinks and food, but I paused to take in the chandelier and double staircase. They definitely made an impression, but I couldn't help thinking that in my regular form, those stairs would have been a hassle, and launching myself from the second floor would be problematic if I didn't want to ruin the chandelier. As a human, though, I could bound up those steps.

"Impressive, isn't it?"

I somehow managed not to jump out of my skin. Stupid peripheral vision—or lack thereof! Pam Mercer stood behind me, almost exactly in the same position she'd taken with the marketing VP. I took a step back, so we stood side by side.

She'd pulled her hair out of her ponytail and brushed it so it fell around her face and shoulders in brown waves. It was thick and a little frizzy, an adorable contrast to the perfectly coifed 'do's of the guests. I could see her shoulders, too. She'd lost the lab coat and her shirt underneath was sleeveless and, I now realized, a little shimmery. A compromise between work and party, then.

"It is," I answered her question. "I was just wondering what it'd be like to slide down the banister."

"I've never done anything like that," she sighed.

"Should we? First time for everything!"

She snickered, but replied, "I'd probably get fired—if I didn't overbalance and break something. I don't think this is that kind of party, anyway. I've got a twenty-minute break, so I was going to go raid the buffet table. But I saw you and I wanted to thank you for laughing at my joke. I regretted it as soon as it left my mouth."

"Nonsense! If they didn't get the Heterodyne reference, they should have at least appreciated the twist on the Arthur C. Clarke quote."

"Thank you!" Her voice rang with enthusiasm. "You read *Girl Genius*?"

"I'm talking to Girl Genius," I replied playfully. The other couple pairings were all walking arm in arm, so I offered Pam mine and we headed into the ballroom.

Historical registry or no, I think they knocked out some walls to make the ballroom. It was huge, dim, and loud. Before us and to the right stood buffet tables and bars, semi-crowded, and to the left, past some tall round tables, was a very crowded dance floor. TVs along all the walls played commercials for products, their narrative competing with the tunes the DJ pumped out. Lights were flashing in multiple colors and a disco ball caused brilliant white speckles to dance on all the surfaces.

The noise and lights overwhelmed me, and I hesitated at the threshold. Fortunately, Pam seemed to have the same reaction. We looked at each other, and a feeling of kindred spirits flashed between us. Then, with mutual shrugs, we went to attack the buffet.

We filled our plates with tidbits and found a table toward one edge. There was no escaping the noise, but it was a little darker and less psychedelic there, although I had an oppressive view of the TV behind her. It played scenes of a man with a receding hairline rubbing some kind of lotion into his scalp, alternating with scenes of a half-naked man running through the woods and howling at the moon. The commercial ended with Baldy—now sporting a full head of hair—in the arms of a beautiful woman who was running her fingers through his luscious locks. He grinned ferally at the camera.

The caption read: *Pelt—unleash the wolf in you.*

I guess I gaped. Pam turned around and made a disparaging noise at the commercial. I managed to hear it, so she hadn't been trying to be quiet about her opinion. She turned back to me. "Yeah, that's next on the market. I think it makes hair tonic look cringey, but I'm not in Marketing. So are you a reporter then? 'Cause we had several reporters in the groups that went through, and they almost all asked corporate questions."

"Nope," I said as I took a casual look around. Yeah, there was McGrue, all dolled up but on the dance floor rather than asking annoying questions. There was no pattern to her movements, or anyone else's for that matter. Just a lot of gyrating bodies twisting around at random. Nothing like the videos I'd watched. Was this how Mundanes danced in the wild? How disappointing.

"Don't like reporters, then?"

"Some are okay," I hedged, then to get her back on track, I said, "I'm actually applying for a modeling job, and got invited. Maybe this is some kind of audition for me? I didn't want to ask too many questions. I mean, why turn down free food and a chance to network?"

She blinked with surprise. "A model. Wow. I can see it. I mean, of course I can see it. Look at you! It's just... Don't get me wrong, but you seem really smart."

She was so cute, getting all flustered. I reared back with theatrical indignance. "I'm extremely smart—and devastatingly attractive."

She laughed. "Are you sure you haven't sampled our perfume?"

"No. I'm just arrogant." I gave her a moment to laugh, then said, "But that raises a question. How can a perfume make someone more confident? Aside from smelling nice?"

She paused to sip her cola. "See? Good question. You know that scents affect people, right?"

"Sure, but I thought it was more basic—hunger, disgust, the desire to mate." Before she could blush, I added, "Sometimes a scent triggers a memory, too."

She pointed at me with a bruschetta. "I knew you were Faerie. 'Desire to mate,' absolutely. That's one of the strongest reactions, at least in humans. I'm not sure about the other sapients."

"I thought it was mostly pheromones, though, which does not explain how you can claim to bottle confidence."

"Flowers, chocolate, scented candles—they're used to set a mood for a reason. But back to confidence. It turns out (not like it's a surprise) that feelings of confidence and sexiness are not all that different."

"Oh?" I asked doubtfully. "I know plenty of confident people who don't feel sexy. Like clergy." I stopped myself before I said Grace's name. "Or parents around their kids."

"Again: *similar*, but not the same. It's all about degree and intent, much of which we have conscious control over, which is why the perfume works for work or, um, play. But biochemically..."

She launched into an explanation I half understood but which she had complete confidence in. I listened intently, committing every word to memory in case it proved important. I also noted how she was leaning toward me, a perfect demonstration of the link between confidence and sexiness.

But something twigged in her, and the confidence shattered like a glass wall. She sat back, suddenly embarrassed. "I'm sorry. That was probably more than you ever wanted to know."

"I'm extremely intelligent, remember?" I teased. "I caught most of it. Besides, I like your passion."

She smiled but didn't meet my eyes. An awkward silence grew between us as I struggled to find a segue to the topic of Emmitt, and she watched the dancers. I followed her gaze.

A large group near us had begun moving in coordinated steps, stepping, clapping, and shaking in tandem. I felt a pang of envy and longing. I missed my dragon kin and our complex dances.

I gave in to my impulse and grabbed Pam by the hand. "Come on!"

"I don't know how!" she protested but let me drag her along.

"So? Neither do I."

Several dancers obviously knew the steps, but plenty of others joined in, learning as they went. We found spots in the middle where we could see dancers no matter which way the group faced. We fumbled at first, but it didn't take long to catch on. After all, I was a dragon; we danced in great, wild, complex patterns in three dimensions that included streams of fire. Our displays awed and sometimes terrified those fortunate enough to witness our antics.

This, this was stomping and clapping, and twisting one's hips, a little hop. Simplistic and repetitive.

I loved every minute of it.

Too soon, the song ended, replaced by something slower. People clapped briefly then paired up or left the dance floor.

Pam stood, awkward and unsure.

I didn't want to leave the floor and the feeling of being part of the group, participating in something bigger than myself. Besides, the DJ was playing, "Through Millennia."

"I love this song." I held out my hands inviting her to waltz.

Or something like that. We shuffled in a tight circle, arms in close so as to not knock into anyone else. Pam blushed and watched the other dancers rather than me. I felt her palms start to sweat. Was she comparing us to the dancers around us? Regardless, I could sense her self-confidence starting to crumble.

"So what kind of scientist is in charge of 'verifying the integrity of the scientific analysis'?" I asked.

She laughed. "You have a good memory! Really, that's Marketing for 'she's a lab tech in QA.' I'm still working on my master's at See-sull." She pronounced the college name "CSU-LL" like a local. "I have an entry-level job. I'm the pariah that has to test for allergens and adverse reactions."

A man near the edge of the dance floor led his partner into a spin. I'd seen how to do that in a video, so I tried it with Pam. She moved out, spun, and returned to my... was it an embrace? We were certainly close. I'd never embraced a human. I'd pounced on them, even held them screaming and struggling between my claws while I soared a hundred feet into the air. But cradling someone gently in my arms as we swayed back and forth was a new experience. Suddenly, I was feeling a little shy. I wanted and dreaded to look straight into her eyes and opted to look over her shoulder instead.

Still, I could hardly waste this chance for gathering information. "Why 'pariah'?"

She let go of my hand to crook her finger at me. I leaned down.

She whispered in my ear, "Animal testing."

Her breath against my skin sent a shiver down my spine. For a moment, I didn't know how to react. Fortunately, she had launched into an explanation about how Mundane testing methods didn't give definitive results for the Faerie/Mundane products.

"It's that nebulous 'Faerie tech' factor, along with some serious proprietary information rules. QA is not even allowed to know some of the ingredients in the perfume, and we're in charge of its safety, can you believe it?"

That news broke through my spell. "Wait, what?"

"It's not unusual. Cosmetics, shallow as it may seem, is a highly competitive industry. I can't blame them for being careful. What we're doing really is revolutionary. So, we have to go Old School. We try to be as humane as possible, of course."

The song ended and moved to a faster one. She looked at her watch. "Shoot! My break ended! Can we... um, take this up again when my shift ends?"

"I'm not sure when I'm leaving," I said. The charm around my ankle had not alerted me to anything, but I had hardly mingled yet.

"Well, you're stuck here until eleven at least," Pam told me. "Our CEO has a board meeting, and he doesn't want anyone to leave until he's made his big presentation and announced who is wearing Persuasion at the party. He comes at ten-thirty and the coat room doors are locked until then."

"Wow. Ego much?" I led her off the dance floor to our table.

She laughed. "It's all marketing in this biz. Get used to it. Still..."

She snagged a waitress—Sister Grace, now in a blond wig and a long black dress—and asked to borrow a pen. She pulled up my sleeve and wrote her phone number on my arm.

"Aren't you supposed to do that on the hand?" Grace asked. I caught a tone of disapproval in her fake accent. She glanced at me long enough to make sure I understood who she was disappointed with.

Pam didn't notice. "Too easy to smudge on hands." She passed back the pen to Grace with thanks in the sweetest way possible.

Then she turned back to me. "So... Hopefully, I'll see you later?"

We did the very awkward start to shake then end up fast-hugging, and she skipped off. Like actually skipped. It drew a couple of amused looks.

But not from my partner.

"Enjoying yourself, sir?" she asked stiffly.

I didn't think the "help" should take such a tone with guests.

I replied with equal stiffness. "I am, thank you."

"Canapé?"

Her tray held pieces of cantaloupe wrapped in ham. Definitely not a canapé. I got the hint: *Concentrate on work.*

Which I was doing, thank you very much.

I told her, "I'd better pace myself. Apparently, we're all locked in here for the next two hours or more. Did you know that?"

"Oh?"

"Yeah, I guess they're holding our coats hostage to the CEO's speech."

"Hm. I'll let my manager know. Enjoy your evening." She moved on without waiting for my answer.

Was that snark from my nun? I forced myself not to react or to follow her with my eyes. Granted, this was not the first time she'd chided me, but usually, I knew what I'd done wrong when she did.

Maybe her feet hurt. Mine were starting to. Why did humans enjoy footwear so much?

I headed to the bar to get a drink and find a place to sit when a light touch on my shoulder made me jump. Cursing my vision and hiding my thoughts with a smile, I turned to see an attractive blonde with eyes so blue they had to be contacts.

"I'm Janet. Let's dance."

My feet didn't hurt so much after all. I took her hand and we wound our way to the dance floor.

Chapter Nine:
Five Minutes Ducking Cassandra

An hour later, I'd learned that uncoordinated dancing was a lot of fun, after all. Janet turned out to be an excellent dancer and a good teacher. I was glad we were deep in the crowd away from the buffet, though. I wasn't sure Grace would approve of some of the moves she taught me.

It wasn't all fun and games. I learned Janet was in Marketing and had not heard of Siobhan.

"But it's not uncommon. We get some people like that—they get hired and then the first day, are transferred somewhere else or discover they aren't a good fit. We have very demanding standards. You'll fit just fine," she said as she leaned back against me and caressed my jaw. The action made me feel...feral.

I had a sudden vision of Grace blowing her top, and took Janet's hand to spin her around a couple of times before letting her go at a more respectable distance.

She introduced me to Christie and Matt who were both in Sales. They didn't have any useful information for me, but they could dance. Foursome dancing was even more fun than just dancing with Janet, especially since no one seemed to care who was dancing with whom. I snuck in a couple of dragonlike moves that they declared "Fae da way."

They'd all had a few drinks, and as we moved to a table to take a break, Mark grabbed a couple of champagne flutes off a passing tray and gave one to me, declaring I needed to catch up. While they watched the dance floor, I stuck a finger in the liquid. The nail stayed clear, so I stuck my finger in my mouth. As a dragon, I had a keen sense of taste and could identify a large number of drinks as well as if anything had been added that altered the taste. It didn't always work, but I'd promised Grace to be extra careful.

All my human tastebuds picked up was a sweetness mixed with the unique sting of alcohol.

I took a sip, planning on nursing it for the night. The warmth of it flowing down my throat surprised me. It was almost like breathing fire. I took another larger sip, vowing to stop after that one. I had no idea what the metabolism of this body was like. For all I knew I was the ultimate lightweight.

Janet had turned to watch me. She leaned forward, focused. Was I drooling?

"You're so intense," she said. "The way you dance. The way you drink. I like a man who knows how to savor each sensation."

Okay. I suddenly felt warmer than even the room or the champagne could account for. "A friend of mine accused me of being a sensualist."

She shrugged, and I was momentarily distracted by how the motion of her shoulders made the fabric of her dress shimmer. "A little sensualism isn't such a bad thing, is it? I mean, that's what we're selling, right? The enjoyment of physicality?"

"That's a good point." I toasted her with my glass. One glass of champagne couldn't hurt, right?

She reached out and stroked my hand. "Why don't we take our drinks somewhere quieter and discuss this further?"

I was scrambling for a good reason not to and wondering why I was resisting when Cassandra stepped up behind Janet and addressed me.

"Victor! I have found you at last. Have you been enjoying yourself?"

"Immensely," I told her. I smiled at her, then Janet.

But smooth as my silky shirt—which Cassandra was eying suspiciously—Janet slid her hand off mine and left without a word. Cassandra took her place, including setting her hand over mine.

I may not have read the FTW organization chart, but any dragon would recognize the hierarchy taking place. Cassandra was more than a recruiter, then.

"Well, I hope you're ready to escape the noise for a bit," she told me as if we had already been deep in conversation. "There are some people upstairs I want you to meet."

"Upstairs?"

She caressed my fingers and hand lightly, which sent some interesting tingles up my arm. "Mmm-hmm. I've told them all about you. They're very excited to meet you."

She ran a finger playfully along the bridge of my nose.

Why not? I wouldn't get any more information out of the people around her now that the Uberfemme had laid claim to me. With a small shrug, I slid from my spot by the table and offered her my arm. I was going to get to ascend the famed staircase, after all.

But as we stepped into the brighter and quieter rotunda, dragon-me snatched hold of my brain. How many times had I unwittingly been caught in a pretty trap? Besides, I'd promised Grace I'd be careful.

I paused at the bathrooms near the stairs.

"Mind if I freshen up first?" I'd heard humans use that phrase dozens of times, yet it sounded odd coming out of my mouth.

She looked me over, making some kind of judgment I didn't understand. "Do you need a toothbrush?"

Did I? Brushing teeth would buy me time. "Yes?"

She pulled one out of her satin clutch. I noticed it matched her champagne gown. The package declared it a one-use disposable with toothpaste in the bristles. I recognized the brand—not FTW.

"I have a lot of experience with models," she said by explanation—which didn't help me understand why she had a new toothbrush in her purse at all, but I took it with thanks. Before she released me, however, she said, "This is not the color I chose for you."

"No," I agreed. "The gold one looked great, but this one called to me." I gave her what I hoped was my I'm-nicer-when-I-get-my-way grin. It was a good one as a dragon, but I didn't know how well it worked without all my extra teeth.

Apparently, it did well enough. She ran two fingers from my throat and down my chest to the first buttoned button. For a moment, my brain locked up as my body sent it all kinds of pleasing and confusing signals.

"At least you learned one lesson," she purred.

I could really get used to this level of attention. "I can be taught," I purred back.

She smirked. It was a dangerous smirk. I could respect dangerous. "I'll bet you can. Third room on the left, near the elevator. You have five minutes."

"It'll be worth it," I replied, belatedly thinking no one in the history of flirtation ever said that about a bathroom break. Ah, well. I had a toothbrush.

I watched her saunter away until she'd ascended the stairs until it blocked her line of vision to me.

Then I dashed back into the ballroom. I scanned the buffet area for Grace's wig, wishing I had my beautiful, long neck. I didn't see her anywhere!

Four minutes.

I grabbed the first waiter that came near. His name tag said Soleil. I guess his parents liked the circus. "Have you seen a waitress, shoulder-length blond hair, green eyes—like emeralds—long dress?"

"If you're hitting on her, don't bother. She's married or something," he answered boredly.

"She's my ride. Look, can you let her know I'm in a meeting upstairs, third room on the left?"

"Yeah, sure. Canapé?"

They were actual canapés. I took one. Then a thought struck me. "Hang on. Did you hit on—"

But he'd already moved on.

Two and a half minutes.

I dashed back to the bathroom to make my excuse legit.

Chapter Ten:
Seven Deadly Sins Shoutout:
Envy
OR
Seven Minutes in the Closet
with Kitty

As ritzy as the Porter Mansion claimed to be, you'd think they'd splurge on towels instead of anemic air dryers.

At four minutes, forty-five seconds, I hurried out of the men's room, trying to shake out the water from under my nails and wondering if brushing my teeth had been a good idea. I'd tried to get the toothpaste on a nail first and it didn't reveal anything, but I didn't know if my polish worked for anything but alcohol. At least I could be assured there were no spells.

Lost in thought about potentially poisoning myself for the sake of pearly whites and minty breath, I crashed right into a woman who was exiting the ladies' room.

No wings for counterbalance. No tail for support. I reached out and grabbed the first thing available. The lady did the same.

We ended up arm in arm.

"Whoa! Careful!" she chided.

"Sorry. I—"

I looked up into the face of Kitty McGrue, reporter for the Los Lagos Gazette and perpetual pain in my tail.

And she looked amazing.

My brain shorted out and started a reboot.

She blinked at me with that same kind of blank, surprised expression I felt on my own face.

"Hi." Her voice was breathy, not at all like her usual acerbic tone. My ears liked it. She smelled as good as she looked.

"Hi," I managed. My neurons were spinning in a holding pattern that somehow timed with the pounding of all my pulse points.

Someone beside us cleared her throat. We were blocking the door to the ladies' room.

Somehow, we made the decision together to move to a more out-of-the-way spot under the stairs.

"I'm Kitty," she started.

But my brain had finally kicked in. "I know who you are. What are you doing here?"

Her voice regained its acid tone. "Excuse me?"

Fewmets! "Victor" didn't know her. Why wasn't I thinking clearly around her? Maybe the toothpaste was drugged. I scrambled for a plausible explanation for her. "Sorry. I mean I know your work for the *Gazette*. I'm Victor DiGiorgio."

For once, I was glad for the awful name. Not only was it easy to remember, but the image of St. George laughing at my discomfiture helped clear my head.

Sort of. She ducked her head shyly, and I found myself feeling warm and protective and weirdly cuddly. Then her gaze turned keen. "Wait. I've seen you. At the job fair, right?"

"Right!" Grateful for another reason to focus on my annoyance and not on her fingers toying with her hair, I added, "You published a very flattering photo of me with a very unflattering caption. I know they don't assign you puff pieces. So what's your story?"

She tsked in surprise. "You're presumptuous."

I was also running out of time. Why was I lingering here? Cassandra would be looking for me soon. Still, maybe Kitty could give me some insight into what to expect if I followed my FTW keeper up the magnificent staircase.

"A friend of mine took a job at Fulfill the Wish Cosmetics and went missing as soon as she got to the Mundane. No one claims to know about her. Is that the story?"

Someone passed us by then, and we fell silent. At least it wasn't Cassandra.

Kitty stepped closer to me. "You mean, Siobhan Miraculi? Are you thinking...?"

"I don't know what to think," I said. I meant it on several levels. I was getting distracted by her hair. I'd never seen it styled like that. Was it as silky as mine? I clenched my fists against the urge to touch it.

One mystery at a time. I bullied my mind to the issue at hand. "If you're not looking for Siobhan, then what are you looking for?"

"Why would I tell you anything?"

"You help me; I'll help you. Tell me what to look for. I'll be your inside source." McGrue could never resist an inside source.

She frowned with uncertainty. Then her shoulders slumped. I knew it. She didn't have a clue what she was looking for.

She said, "I'm not sure, but there's something not kosher about this company's sudden rise in popularity. My Kitty senses are tingling..."

Suddenly, my senses were tingling, and not just from her nearness. I'd caught the faint sound of a door above us being opened and closed and more definite footsteps heading to the stairs. As a dragon, I'd have been able to tell the approximate height, weight, gender, and footwear of the person. As Victor, all I knew was the person wore heels.

That was enough for me. With a tight curse, I pulled Kitty into a dark corner out of the line of sight of our approaching intruder.

"What?" Kitty started in surprise, then shut up. At least she caught on fast.

I crouched behind her while watching past her shoulder. "Stay still."

Cassandra rounded the bend, heading toward the bathrooms. She moved casually, but with purpose. She waltzed into the men's room without any hint of modesty. A moment later, she exited, looking both ways. I ducked lower. Kitty pulled out her phone and pretended to take a selfie.

A moment later, I heard a cluck of annoyance and the sound of Cassandra's heels clicking toward the ballroom. I let out a breath I hadn't even known I was holding.

"My eyes are up here," Kitty said, albeit quietly.

"What? Oh, sorry." Cassandra would need a couple of minutes to search the ballroom. I stood up.

"Avoiding someone? Cassandra, maybe?" Kitty asked, and there was a smugness in her voice.

"I don't like your tone," I scolded, then added, "She said there was a meeting upstairs she wanted me to attend."

"Upstairs. Where the bedrooms are."

"There could be suites," I protested, but mentally kicked myself for not finding a blueprint of the B&B. "Did you happen to see anyone else heading upstairs, preferably dowdy old men who reeked of money and power?"

"Did you really expect some?"

"Believe it or not, this is a new experience for me," I snarked back. I was hyper-aware of how her superior tone grated on my nerves. Hyper-aware of her nearness to me. I wanted to ask her to step back, but I felt a challenge in her proximity, and dragons faced challenges. I could handle McGrue.

For some reason, my words seemed to soften her attitude. She took a half-step back without my asking. "Well, if it's any consolation, for all that this is supposed to be about wooing investors, I'm not seen anyone head upstairs with business on their mind—dowdy or not. In fact, I've not seen a lot of investor types at all.

Lots of influencers, sure. I wish I could get a hold of the guest list."

"Bet it's in the office behind the reception desk with the coats."

She rolled her eyes. "I did think of that, but they've locked the doors."

The increased distance between us helped. I could breathe again, and that made me feel generous. "Would lockpicks help?"

She raised her brows, surprised and impressed. Figured that all my magnificence as a dragon didn't faze her but a hint of the criminal dazzled her.

"Are you a Boy Scout or a felon?"

She seemed like either answer would satisfy her. Unfortunately, that was more backstory for Victor than I'd come up with. "Does it matter?"

Her grin grew wider. I found myself grinning back. Despite myself, I liked the dazzled Kitty with her eyes full of mischief.

I looked back over her shoulder. The coast was clear. I took her hand, and we dashed to the coat room. We ducked under the reception desk, which was just a low wall supporting a counter and big enough to hide both of us if we tucked in our legs. We giggled.

Me, giggling with Kitty? I wanted to slap my own face. Instead, I reached into my sock. "Ready for a little larceny?"

"The perfect date."

I opened the case, then paused. I knew how to use the tools, but I'd always used them with my prehensile tail. Could I do it with fingers, and quickly enough to avoid being seen?

Fortunately, Kitty took my hesitation as an invitation.

"Such a gentleman," she teased, snatching up the tools. She crouched in front of the lock. The high-cut panel of her skirt caught on one heel, revealing the curve of one long leg. Had I known how trim her legs were? I must have. So why was I noticing with such intensity now?

She almost beat my best time opening the lock.

"Were you a Girl Scout or a felon?" I asked as we crawled into the room.

"Both."

I stood up fast and shut the door, plunging us into darkness except for the dim parallel lines of the far window. To the right stood racks of coats, I knew, and between them and the now-closed door absorbing all the sound, the room was quiet. I could just make out Kitty's outline, back to me, her hand reaching for the wall.

No. For the light switch.

I surged forward and pulled her hand away, hissing, "The window."

Or at least, I think I said something. The moment I'd grabbed her wrist, she'd turned to look at me, and her hair had brushed against my skin. It was as soft as I'd imagined. I stood frozen, mesmerized by the feeling. I inhaled deeply but it did nothing to abate the sudden dizziness I felt.

Kitty let out a small "oh." Then she cleared her throat and whispered more confidently. "Right. Window. Are there drapes?"

I looked in the direction of the slatted lines and tried to remember. "No. Just the miniblinds."

"Great. Got a penlight in your other sock, not-a-Boy-Scout?"

"Stare at the darkest corner you can find and let your eyes adjust."

We stood there, staring at the deepest nothing we could find. Listening to our breathing, feeling a strange, warm tension flowing between us.

"We have to stop meeting like this," she joked quietly. I didn't know how to reply. My brain was starting to lock up—or rather, to ratchet my thoughts to simple awareness of the scent of her hair, the softness of her skin.

"You can let go of my hand," she whispered. "I won't turn on the light."

"Oh. Right." I didn't want to move—or rather, I did want to move, but it was to bury my face against the back of her neck. What a weird impulse, but I almost felt greedy to do it.

Her smug giggle finally broke the spell, and I let her go. She slid her fingers along mine as she lowered her arm.

"I can see shadows and shapes now. Why don't you look along the wall for a desk or shelf and I'll check the coats," she suggested.

"No one's going to put the registry in their jacket," I protested, grateful to be talking about the mission again.

"I'm going to look for other clues."

"Like what? A competitor's lipstick? Maybe you should tell me about this felony of yours."

"Sorry. You have to earn that information."

She started down between two rows, so I moved forward, one hand on the wall and my feet shuffling so I didn't trip on anything. Stupid human vision—on top of everything else, it's no good for the dark. I made out a bookshelf and ran my fingers over the shelves. Hats, purses, a couple of figurines, some galoshes... I stood and continued on.

"Oooo!" Kitty sing-songed quietly.

"What?" I turned my head in her direction just as my knee cracked against a desk. I caught myself before I fell against it, biting down against the urge to shout in pain. Meanwhile, Kitty purred something about never touching real mink before.

"Super soft."

There was nothing soft about the pain in my knee. If I'd had my real hands, my claws would have gouged the desk. Instead, the soft pads of my fingers rubbed against the faux leather of the guest book.

"Found it," I said through clenched teeth. I took a breath, releasing the tension in my body. The pain in the knee throbbed but lessened. "Got a camera?"

I felt along the desk. It held a lamp with a half-pipe hood that let the light shine directly down on the paper. I took a chance and clicked it on and off. Yep, a nice, direct light, not too bright, either. Someone was into Edison bulbs. I clicked it back on and started flipping through pages, thankful I still had my photographic memory. Grace had given me a charm with a tracking spell. If by any chance Emmitt was here and I could find his coat, I could plant it, and we could find him that way.

Dimly, I heard Kitty making her way through the coats.

Emmitt... Emmitt... Come on, Emmitt...

Something velvety and plush rubbed against the back of my neck. I'd have jumped out of my skin if I hadn't been distracted by the chills it sent down my spine. Even so, I spun around fast.

Kitty was right in front of me, a phone in one hand and a mink stole in the other. She rested her wrist on my shoulder and tickled me with the stole.

"I thought we were looking for clues," I said sternly, but I couldn't help leaning my cheek against the soft fur. Guess I was a sensualist, after all.

"Oh, you likey the mink," she sing-songed, and for some reason that made me smirk. I much preferred her silly, coy voice. "Besides, I found something else."

She waved the phone where I could see the screen more clearly.

She giggled. "What idiot leaves their phone in their coat?"

Me. She was holding my phone.

"Let me see." As I reached for it, she stuck her hand behind her back. I followed, stepping closer and putting one arm around her.

I thought I'd been close to people today. Kitty and I stood so near to each other we shared the same breaths.

"You planned that," I said. My lips brushed against hers with each word.

"I'm in a dark closet with the hottest guy at the party," she murmured as she played the mink along my neck and down the open part of my shirt. "What did you think would happen?"

I didn't have an answer for that. Electricity like I'd never felt before gathered around us, a current flowing through the mink, from my hand on her back, between our nearly touching lips. I could barely concentrate through the buzzing.

"Give me the phone," I said, though I barely remembered why it mattered. I brushed my lips against hers. The electricity surged in response.

"Make me," she said and kissed me in earnest.

If flying through a cloudy sky and feeling the mist was a feeling I savored, it still didn't compare to the excitement of flying through a thunderstorm. The combination of danger and the tingle of electricity across my wings. I'd never felt anything as exhilarating.

Until now.

And I wanted more.

My arms tightened around her.

Suddenly, the door flew open, bringing a blast of music and light. A figure stood, sharply silhouetted against the brightness.

I acted on instinct. I growled.

Out toward the ballroom, people were cheering.

Kitty leaned her forehead against my chest and giggled.

The woman in the doorway, however, did not find it funny.

"Vurnerrah!" Sister Grace exclaimed.

Chapter Eleven:
Saturday Night Fever

"Vurnerrah, have you lost your mind?"

"Grace?"

Her exclamation was like being tossed into the snow—or maybe being blasted by lightning. Regardless, it snapped me back to my senses.

"Kitty?" I jerked away from her, or as least as far as I could. I was already backed against the desk.

Kitty stepped back, too, a natural reaction to being caught in the act, I suppose. But then she looked from me to Grace then back to me. "Vurnerrah?" she asked.

Then her voice grew disgusted and accusatory. "Vern?"

Now she truly leaped back from me.

I felt my face heat up. "Kitty. I—Ow!"

Grace had stormed into the room and pinched my earlobe between two of her knuckles. I had no idea her fingers were that strong.

"Shame on you!" she scolded Kitty and then marched out of the room, my ear in tow. The rest of me had no choice but to follow. She whistled, and my coat flew off the hanger and into her free hand.

Fortunately, no one was around to witness her actions or my embarrassment. The CEO had begun his speech, and everyone had crowded into the ballroom, its doors shut tight. She stopped at the doors leading outside and shoved my jacket and the car keys at me.

"The car is in the back. Go straight there and wait. Talk to no one."

"But—"

"Go straight to the car and speak to no one until I get there," she sang, and I felt the compulsion come upon me.

Glaring daggers at her, I threw on my jacket and did as I was told. She'd just used a cantrip on me. *Me!* That marked a level of fury I'd never seen in her, and I'd thought I'd seen her at her worst. If I could detect magic, I bet I'd find it circling her like a tornado, maybe even throwing sparks.

I didn't want to raise suspicion by turning on the car, since I didn't know how long she'd be. I donned my seat belt, locked the doors, and hunched up, getting colder and grumpier by the minute. It couldn't have been more than ten minutes when Grace showed up, a duffel bag slung over her shoulder. Nonetheless, my teeth were chattering, and it took two tries to unlock the door. She didn't comment but tossed her duffel in the back and started the car.

We drove in silence down the dark mountain road, the car warming as much from the steam rising off my best friend as from the heater. By the time we'd made it to the edge of town, I'd stopped shivering and Grace no longer strangled the steering wheel. Still, when we got to town, she started taking turns at random. At Main, she pressed on the accelerator, running a light just as it turned red, then taking a sharp right into a narrow alley, nearly clipping a trash can.

"What are you doing?" I shouted.

"Someone's following us."

"What?" I twisted around, looking through all the windows, straining to see anything that might indicate a car. I even opened the window and looked above us for a drone. All I saw were slick, empty streets, and lights muted by the falling snow.

"I don't see anyone."

"I can feel their eyes on us."

Had something happened that I'd missed? I reached out to grab her shoulder. "No one's there. It's okay…"

"Don't touch me!" she snapped.

I jerked like she was a hot stove. "Fine! But no one's following us. So calm down. The roads are slick."

She strangled the steering wheel in her grip, but she did ease up on the accelerator, and when we came to a light, she stopped.

I looked once more for a tail, and finding none, turned back to her. "Are you alright?"

"Are you drunk?" she responded.

So this was about me again? "No. I had one glass of champagne. That's it."

"Did you test it?"

"Of course!" Chagrined as I was, I did not like her tone. I was the one who had coached her about testing every drink. I'd even tested my toothpaste! I started to mention the toothpaste when she slapped the steering wheel.

"Then what were you doing?" she shouted.

"I don't know! Humaning is harder than I thought!"

The light turned green, and she accelerated. Gently. I guess I had reassured her about us not being followed. Now, she reserved her frustration and angry energy for me.

"Do you have any idea how frantic I was? Soleil told me you found a ride and left!"

"Soleil is an idiot," I asserted. "I told him *you* were my ride and...hang on. Did he hit on you?" I felt a sudden urge of possessiveness and anger I didn't even know I'd been harboring inside.

"Vurnerrah, focus! We're talking about you."

I shook it off. "Anyway, I said I'd be upstairs, third room *on the left*."

That made things worse. "Upstairs? Where the..." she sputtered rather than say "bedrooms." "What were you planning to do there?"

"How would I know?" I snapped back. Adrenaline made me start explaining at an increasingly rapid pace. "Cassandra said there were people I needed to meet but I stalled and went to find you, and then I ran into Kitty, and she said no dowdy old investors had gone upstairs and I thought it'd be safer to go with her to search for clues."

"Safer? Really? I was searching for you when my mizpah just about burned a hole in my skin! I thought you'd been kidnapped like Siobhan."

I realized then that the room Cassandra was leading me to was right beside the elevator. Could she have had people lying in wait to conk me out and drag me off during the CEO's speech?

"Sorry."

"Sorry? About what? About willingly putting yourself in danger or..." She turned to glare at me. "Kitty McGrue? Really?"

"Well, you weren't there!" I retorted, then realized how that sounded. "To search for clues, I mean. I was checking the register for Emmitt's name, and Kitty was searching the coats and then she started playing with a mink and got close and things got silky and confusing and...electric..."

"Vurnerrah!"

"Sorry!"

I turned my head toward the window. I was shaking again, but this time with adrenaline. I didn't know who I was angry at.

No. I did. I was angry at whoever cursed me, angry at Kitty for being so...confusing, angry at myself for letting things get so out of hand. First, I told her about looking for Siobhan, then I followed her into a dark room? And I kissed her? That should have been gross; why wasn't it gross? I was really angry—and embarrassed—for enjoying it so much. Angry at God for letting this happen...

But why was I angry at Grace?

After a few blocks of tense silence, Grace said, "Vurnerrah. Vern. You don't understand how dangerous what you did was. For all we know, that could be all you needed to..." She stopped herself.

"To what?" I said, even as my brain finished the sentence. When she didn't answer immediately, I began to panic. "To what, Grace? To make this *permanent?*"

"Vern."

"Stop the car!"

"Vern, calm down." But she pulled over into an empty parking lot.

I yanked off the seatbelt and turned to face her fully. "Check me! Check the spell!"

Oh, please, please! I didn't mean it!

"Shh. Vern. I spoke rashly." Even so, she put the car in park and took off her seat belt. The snow reflected the light from the moon and the tall lamps of the parking lot. Her blond wig took up the light like a halo, but her face was in shadow. I didn't know if she was afraid, annoyed, or just wanting to give me peace.

"Check! Please?"

"Breathe. Calm down. I'll check."

Grace paused a few beats to gather her own nerves, then hovered her hands over me, checking the magic that bound me to this ridiculous form. I kept my eyes screwed shut, afraid to see her expression, and prayed as she moved her hands over my head, my face, my shoulders, my pounding heart.

After a fear-filled eternity, I heard her sigh with relief. "It's alright, Vern. The spell is unchanged."

"Oh, thank God!" I slumped, leaning on the center console for support, my elbows stuck awkwardly in the cupholders and my head in my hands. If the next breath wasn't a sob, it was still shaky.

"Thank you, Grace. I'm sorry. You tried to warn me." I breathed through clenched teeth, trying to calm down. Why did human emotions have to be so intense?

"Shhh." She stroked my hair comfortingly. Gradually, I relaxed under her gentle touch.

"I'm sorry I yelled," she said. "I was scared, too, and... I should have realized you weren't acting out of..."

"Hedonism?" I grinned.

"Something like that." She grinned back. Her teeth seemed especially white in the snowlight.

I basked in the warmth of that smile. Things were fine between us again. Better than fine.

Suddenly, I wanted to kiss her. I *really* wanted to kiss her.

From the growing look of dismay on her face, I guessed she wanted to kiss me, too.

I swallowed hard and sat back. "Maybe you should take me to the rectory."

"That's a good idea." She had the car in gear and was peeling out of the parking lot before I had my seatbelt back on.

We were blessedly close to the church. Even so, the awkward push-and-pull tension between us grew as thick as the snow that had started to fall.

Grace parked in front of the garage but didn't turn off the engine. I got out without saying anything. We didn't look at each other. But I did watch from the corner of the garage as she pulled away. I felt a queasiness in my stomach and a heaviness in my heart. Maybe Father Rich would have a suggestion.

Or maybe he'd say, "I told you so."

Great. Now I could add trepidation to my mix of emotions. I sighed, feeling resigned—yet another emotion, just stirring around in my stomach. I hated being human. I stumped my way to the rectory porch.

I shook the snow off my hair and stamped my feet before ringing the bell. The Hallelujah Chorus did not make me feel any better; what I wanted to hear were Father's footsteps coming down the stairs. I waited. Rang again. Nothing. All the windows were dark, I realized.

I moaned.

Back out to the garage. Peek in the windows. His car was gone. Figured. I tried the garage doors; despite my earlier objections, I'd rather sleep there than outside or even worse, go back to the lair with Grace. The doors were locked tight.

Grumbling, I marched back to the porch, trying not to slip in the snow in my fancy party shoes. I reached into my pocket.

Kitty still had my phone.

I howled at the cloudy sky, and it sounded puny and human.

I had no idea a being could get so cold, and I'd lived through ice ages. Or more to the point, I'd slept through ice ages. Dragons had the lovely ability to sleep through uncomfortable or boring eras, a talent I wish I had retained. Tucked into a corner of Father's porch with my knees up to my chest and my coat tented around me, I was ready to see if I could recapture that skill.

I don't know how long I'd been dozing before I heard an urgent, "Sir? Sir? Are you alright?"

I forced my head up and my eyes to open. It was harder than I expected it to be. Maybe I could hibernate, after all.

Father stared worriedly into my face. "Vern?"

"Where have you been?" I wanted to snarl, but it came out, "whurrhuverrr-chatter-chatter-growl."

"Vern. Oh, my gosh. Come on. Let's get you in."

Soon, I was on the couch in front of the fireplace, dressed in Father's pajamas and buried under blankets, with warm towels wrapped around my hands and feet. I'd gone from cold and numb to shivering and spikey. My fingers and toes seemed to burn from the inside. How did humans survive all this?

"You get used to it," Father said as he gave me a tumbler of hot tea with a straw so I could hold the cup in my lap. "And generally, we don't sit in freezing temperatures if we can avoid it. Why didn't you call someone?"

"Kitty has my phone," I took a sip of tea. It was heavily laced with honey and warmed my esophagus better than the champagne. Who knew an esophagus could get cold?

"Kitty? Kitty McGrue?" Then he asked warily, "Is there something you want to tell me?"

Still sipping the tea and warming with shame as well, I shook my head.

"Something you want to confess?"

I nodded.

Bless that man. His face went neutral, and he rose to get his stole without a comment.

I called after him. "You're going to have to walk me through this. I have no idea how it works for a human."

Long story short...

- Flirting with pretty girls: Not a sin.
- Breaking into a locked room: Not a mortal sin since I didn't destroy or steal anything, but definitely illegal. (Same as for dragons.)
- Kissing Kitty McGrue...

"Why did you kiss her?" Father asked.

"I don't know. Curious, maybe?"

"You don't like her."

"Apparently, as Victor, I do." I couldn't keep the sardonic tone out of my voice.

"Were you planning on doing anything more than kissing?"

"Like what?"

I felt like Father should be rolling his eyes, but he asked calmly, "Where were your hands?"

I thought back. It was a blur now, but a pleasant one. "Hmmm. Her back. Her hair. She has thick, soft hair."

My hands moved at the memory of touching it.

Father was not interested in her hair. "Just her back? You're certain?"

"Yeah. Why...?"

Then it clicked.

I yelped and almost dropped my cup. "Oh! No! Ugh."

"Alright. Kissing a pretty woman isn't, of itself, a sin, but in your case, it's definitely dangerous. I'm not sure you're completely in control of your...curiosity. I think you should keep your distance from attractive ladies."

I nodded. "Social distancing. Got it."

"Wearing a mask might not be a bad idea. But if you are in a similar situation, I suggest you remind yourself of the adage, 'Curiosity killed the cat.' It's not Biblical, but it is easy to remember."

The tea had started to sit heavy and sour in my stomach despite the honey. I muttered the phrase to show I'd heard.

"Anything else?"

"I...wanted to kiss Grace."

"Sister Grace?"

I wanted to snap, "Of course, Sister Grace!" but I knew he was making a point. "Yes."

"But you didn't?"

"No."

"That's why you were on my doorstep in the middle of the night during a snowstorm?" I felt like his tone was approving despite his attempt to stay neutral as he asked. That comforted me some.

"Yeah."

"It's the indulging of a desire that constitutes a sin. You're not daydreaming about kissing Sister Grace, are you?"

"Of course not. That would be..." I searched for the word, but none in the Mundane language came close to what I wanted to say. I finally settled on "disrespectful."

"It's good that you understand that," he said, and he gave me my penance.

I whispered my prayers as he cleaned up. They hurt my throat and made my nose feel bigger. Was that normal for human penance? I was starting to feel a little woozy, too. Now that my body wasn't all pins and needles, it had started to ache in a different way.

When Father returned with his own cup of tea, I asked, "Do I look different?"

He peered at me closely. "No. Why?"

"I sound different, and I feel...wrong."

He set the back of his hand on my forehead. It was cool. "You feel a little warm. Not surprising. You may have a sore throat. Finish your prayers in your head, and then let's get you upstairs."

After I was tucked into bed with a heating pad and a glass of water on the nightstand and Father was turning out the lights, a thought struck me. "Father?"

He paused, his hand on the switch. "Yes, Vern?"

"I did daydream about kissing Kitty. It kept me warm."

"That's normal. But I'd recommend not indulging such thoughts any further. Curiosity killed the cat."

My eyes were getting heavy. I murmured, "Curiosity killed the cat. Father?"

"Yes, Vern?"

"Humaning is hard."

"Yes, it is, Vern. Yes, it is."

I slept like the dead and woke up dying.

My head pounded as if I'd been on a 15-gallon bender. My throat burned like I'd breathed fire, but I couldn't have, or I wouldn't have the hangover. My eyes felt heavy and weirdly crusty. They'd grown too big for their sockets, or maybe it was my sinuses that had swelled; I couldn't breathe through my nose. Every joint in my body ached.

It could only mean one thing—the spell was going wrong!

I thrashed in my covers and groped blindly at the nightstand. I had to call Grace! Who knew what I was turning into now? I didn't want to be a newt...again. Or worse, an emu. No! Anything but an emu!

I knocked over some books, a chain, and a glass of water, but no phone. Where was my phone?

Oh, no! Kitty had it! I kissed Kitty and she stole my phone and I was going to turn into an emu!

I heard hasty footsteps, and the door flew open.

Father looked at the mess and exclaimed, "For heaven's sake, Vern! What's wrong?"

My brain tumbled with words. I was changing again. The spell had backfired because I'd sinned. I needed Grace. I didn't want to be a flightless bird.

"Help," was all that escaped my tortured throat.

Instead of calling Grace—or at least, 9-1-1—he set the back of his hand on my forehead.

He sighed. "You have a fever."

How could that be when I was shivering? I wanted to protest but my human throat only allowed a whimper.

"Stay calm. I'll be right back."

Then he left me alone to deal with whatever horrors befell me. Fine. If I grew feathers and a bad attitude while he was gone, that was on him.

I held my hands before me and watched intently, but other than wavering in and out of focus, they seemed to stay human.

Wait. What if I was supposed to have feathers? What if my original dragon state had magnificent plumage and my fight with St. George had made me molt and then he took away my memory, so I'd be humbled? Blast you, George! I bet I had beautiful feathers like a peacock and now I have beige skin that gets warm by itself.

"What are you doing?" Father asked when he returned. He wore a mask and gloves and carried a tray with a box, a glass of juice, and a small plastic cup with green liquid in it. I might have recognized it if I weren't so distracted by wondering if my nose was turning into a beak.

"Spell," I croaked. Maybe I'd become a frog? A 180-pound amphibian? "Changing?"

"Are you delirious? Easy, now. It's okay, Vern. You just have a fever. Probably a cold or the flu, but I gotta check you for Covid because if you're positive, that means a lot of upheaval for me."

How could he talk about his upheaval at a time like this? But he handed me the cup of liquid and I swallowed it down. It tasted of licorice and soothed my throat. Next, he pulled a swab on a long stick out of a packet and stuck it up my nose.

I froze, confused by the sensation. How could something in my sinuses tickle my ears and jaw? But Kitty kissed me, and I felt it other places than my mouth.

No! I can't think about Kitty! I'll turn into an emu! Stupid human brain, cockamamie human anatomy! Still better than emus. I don't want skinny brown legs!

"Good job," Father said, and I realized he'd mistaken my frozen panic for submissiveness. I shut my eyes and tried to quell my racing thoughts as he went through the rest of the test.

While we waited, he got me another blanket and put a cold compress on my head.

"If the test is negative, I'm going to go to Mass. Sister Grace will be there, and I'll let her know. She's bringing some clothes for you, anyway."

Clothes? Like the suit, the suit we borrowed from the *funeral ministry?* "I'm dying?"

"No, you're not dying."

"No...beak?"

"No. But I think you are definitely delirious." His watch beeped, and he looked at the Covid test stick. "But at least you don't have Covid, so it's probably just a bad flu. It's going around. You'll be fine in a day or two, promise. The best thing you can do is sleep. I left some orange juice for you on the nightstand. Try not to knock it over, okay?"

It hurt to speak, so I nodded. That hurt only marginally less.

"I'll check on you after Mass," he promised. He collected the books from the floor and put them on the dresser, then picked up the empty cup and took it out with the rest of the detritus on the tray.

I checked my hands for feathers once more and reassured myself that my nose, while human, was still a nose, then shut my eyes.

I slept, took medicine, drank juice, and slept more. At some point, an angel came to me and promised that I wasn't turning into an emu or any other nonaquatic, flightless fowl or their evolutionary predecessors. She couldn't, however, return me to my dragon state or cure my cold.

I didn't know which was more disappointing.

"Be patient, my silly dragon," the angel said. "Rest and be patient."

Chapter Twelve:
Seven Deadly Sins Shoutout:
Lust

I dreamed I was on a dance floor soaring among the clouds, dancing with all the women I met at the party. Lizzie from Little Flowers wore her choir robe cinched around the waist and the zipper partly unzipped, revealing a chain full of Grace's medallions. Mary from the job fair was there, too. I didn't know how she got there, but it didn't matter. That septuagenarian could dance.

They could all dance—like *dragon* dance. We moved in complex, synchronized choreography beyond human capabilities. Their skirts swirled reminiscent of tails and when they flared their arms, the clouds streamed over them like wings. It was glorious. They were glorious, and I was so happy.

Then the dancing grew aggressive. They bumped into me, playfully at first, but quickly, caresses became swipes. Grasps hardened into desperate clutches. I struggled to escape. My feet grew into heavy leather boots before they sank into the dance floor.

From a corner, Kitty McGrue laughed. Wings sprouted from her shoulders, magnificent and wrong. She waved my cell phone at me. Something told me if I tried to run to her, I could escape, but the idea tempted and repulsed me. Her wings were wrong. I didn't understand her wings.

Cassandra scratched me, and brown-gray feathers sprouted from the wound.

Grace! I needed Grace. She'd save me and then my wings would come back and... I didn't know what else, just that I had to find Grace. Maybe if I threw myself off the dance floor, my wings would come back. Then Grace would be there.

I started to shove my way to the edge of the floor, my feet dragging as if through mud. The girls started to screech and beat at me with heavily ringed hands. Then they turned into emus. Then started devolving into velociraptors.

Among the sea of feathers and teeth, I caught a glimpse of a deep blue wimple. Grace!

The dance floor tilted.

"Grace!"

I bolted upright in bed, calling my friend's name. Silence responded. I sat, panting, trying to get my bearings. My eyes scanned the small bedroom wildly. Why was I so angry and unsettled?

It was just a dream. I'm fine.

Then, I paused, bemused, because I actually did feel fine. Father was right. The flu had lasted a few horrifying days, but I'd recovered. I could breathe again!

And I smelled terrible.

I pulled back the covers. I braced myself on the nightstand until my balance returned, but I was less wobbly than during my first few moments as a human. A fresh glass of orange juice waited by the lamp. I drank it down. My pajamas were damp with sweat. Ick.

A pile of clothes waited on the dresser, along with a note. I smiled to see Grace's handwriting.

You do seem determined to have the full human experience, don't you? I tried to heal you, but the magic just bounced off. I don't like that, for a number of reasons. It's time to consult with my order. In the meantime, <u>please be careful</u>! You're frail as any human, and I can't help you.

I suppose that should have scared me, but at the moment, all I felt was a surge of joy. She'd come to visit me! She wasn't mad at me, after all.

She'd also left instructions on how to be a good guest, so as soon as I'd taken a long, hot shower, I stripped the bed and put the dirty linens in the washing machine, then went in search of breakfast.

I set off the fire alarm trying to make scrambled eggs and almost burned my hand again when I tried to grab the iron skillet. Of course, I was also tickled that I could touch Father's iron skillet. I was cooling both hand and pan under cold running water when Father came dashing through the front door and into the kitchen.

I held up the skillet, where my attempt at breakfast now floated. "Sorry. I was trying to feed myself."

Father pursed his lips. "For future reference, you don't include the shells."

"Oh. Right." I'd thought they'd looked wrong.

"Glad to see you're up and about, though." Father turned on the stove vent and cracked a window. Cool air wafted in. Then he took over cleaning the frying pan, telling me to have a seat. "You were really out of it the past two days. Kept going on about emus."

Suddenly, I felt a chill that had nothing to do with the weather or my previous illness. Could I *die* as a human? Grace couldn't help me, she'd said.

"How feverish was I?"

Father must have caught the edge in my voice. "Easy. It was just a bad flu. Your fever didn't get over a hundred and two. It was probably more anxiety than anything else. That was your first flu, right?"

"May it be my last."

Father made us fresh eggs, no shells, while I poured us coffee. At least I knew how to make that. It was hard to mess up with a coffee pod machine.

Between swallows, Father caught me up on what I'd missed. "Grace said she had a new lead to follow, and she wanted to try one more thing for you before going to her order. Apparently, Kitty emailed her something? God knows why, but there was a little snark in her voice when she mentioned Kitty's name."

I grunted. "God knows why" was his way of referring to what I'd told him in Confession. As Rich, he officially did not know why Grace might have a chip on her shoulder, but he thought it important that I realized she had not fully come to terms with that night.

But she'd visited me. She'd tried to heal me. She'd left me a note. It'd be okay. I'd call Grace later. We'd work it out.

Then I groaned. "Does Kitty still have my phone?"

My Rhyde, not Pyitr but an older human who talked about how it made a good retirement job, dropped me off in front of Kitty's house. He didn't offer to wait and was halfway down the block before I'd thought to ask. I sighed. Now, I'd be stuck in the cold until I got another Rhyde. Maybe I'd call Father. He had offered to drive me and go in with me, but I'd insisted I was an adult and didn't need a chaperone, and as he had meetings at the school, he'd relented.

Now, I kind of wished I'd not been so quick to refuse his help. I did not want to face McGrue. I had this sudden vision of her laughing at me, waving my phone in my face while she wore my wings. I shook my head. Stupid fever dreams.

I straightened my shoulders and strode forward. I would not let some presumptuous little human get the best of me. I wore the wings. And I wanted Victor's phone back. I took the steps two at a time.

Her porch had three steps. I awkwardly overstepped the last and almost lost my balance. At least no one saw and I didn't try to use my tail. I told myself to count it as a win as I rang the doorbell.

"What do you want, *Vern?*" Kitty's disembodied voice came from the doorbell. It held all the ire I expected. I could almost feel the hateful glare.

The feeling was mutual. She didn't deserve to wear my wings. "Good morning to you, too. I came for my phone."

A pause. "You're kidding. You're the idiot?"

Just like that, she popped the bubble of anger I'd shielded myself with. I forced myself not to squirm. "I'm not used to pockets, okay?"

That earned me a chuckle. A couple of moments later, the door opened. The draft of warm air felt nice on my face. I caught the scent of coffee, burning wood, and something else that made me think of the party.

Nothing about Kitty resembled the woman I'd joined in the coat closet. She wore an oversized Broncos jersey, yoga pants, and fuzzy slippers. Her hair might have encountered a brush earlier in the day, but now it looked mussed from her running her fingers through it. I wondered if she was researching something, and if it might apply to my case. Another part of me, the traitorous human part, thought she looked adorable.

"That's a new look," I commented, in case my face revealed my thoughts. That might have been a bad idea; I'm not sure I sounded as snarky as I'd intended.

She curled her lip. "New look, really? You should talk."

She took a couple of steps back and waited. "Well? Are you coming in, or shall we continue to heat the outside?"

Confused, I stepped over the threshold and shut the door. "I just want my phone."

"Duh. I just have to remember where I put it. Keep your shirt on."

"I wasn't planning on—"

"Figure of speech!"

"Oh. Right." I said, feeling very stupid, especially since my gaze kept drifting to her as she had bent over to search a junk drawer—or what I assumed was a junk drawer. Maybe it was where she kept the trophies from other times she'd accosted men in small offices.

I should not be thinking about her accosting me that night. I might turn into an emu.

I wandered the other direction toward the living room. It surprised me with its neatness. I'd seen Kitty's office at the Gazette—at least, I think it was an office and not the spot where she dumped papers and coffee cups. This room, though. One wall held a desk, but other than the double monitors, some mail, a notebook, and a cup of writing utensils, it was surprisingly sparse. A modern, gray couch faced a fireplace. Real wood burned in it—pine and, I could now tell, aspen. The crackling soothed me, and I closed my eyes and inhaled deeply.

"What are you doing?" Kitty interrupted me.

"I love fire." I sighed.

I opened my eyes to find her standing in front of me, an inscrutable look on her face. I should have sneered and demanded to know what was wrong now, but the calm of the fire had hold of me. I smiled instead.

Her lips quirked in a half-smile in return. "Yeah. I guess that makes sense."

She held out my phone but yanked it back as I reached for it. At least she didn't put it behind her back. Still, I didn't fall for the same ploy twice.

"McGrue..."

"Don't you think you owe me an apology first?"

It was a good thing the fire had soothed my nerves. I might have said something that I would have had to apologize for later. Instead, I crossed my arms and raised a brow. "Apologize for...?"

She tutted indignantly. "You don't think that at some point, *Vern*, you should have told me the truth about who—what—you were? Like, you know, before we started kissing?"

Damsels and knights, this body had good kinetic memory. Just her saying the word, "kissing" brought back visceral memories of her in my arms. My arms could actually feel the action of reaching out to her.

I fought the desire with simple ire. "I was undercover. I actually am working on a case, a real case, not a nebulous 'something's not kosher about FTW.' And as long as I'm stuck in this body, I'm not Vern. I'm Victor."

I did not impress her. She huffed. "That's the best you can do? Was it part of your cover to *make out* with me? Like you thought, 'I'll be more convincing if I kiss someone I normally despise.' Well, good job. That was one hell of a kiss, Vern."

"Victor!"

"Victor is dead to me! I'm going to call you HuVern."

"HuVern?"

"Yes, HuVern, as opposed to VernDrake, which is you in your annoying but more natural form."

Aargh! Why did she have to be so obstinate? And cute. Why was she cute? And now she had to say something clever. HuVern. Why didn't I think of that?

I took some hasty steps away from her. "For pity's sake, McGrue. I'm not kidding around. A girl's life is at stake, and I got stuck in this form. You think I'm enjoying the downgrade?"

"You were Friday night."

"I'm sorry, alright? I didn't mean to—" I was not saying the words. "—or to be so good at it. We were getting along and you had that dress and your legs and that hair; there was this current between us and..."

I had no idea what I was saying.

I leaned against the back of her couch, defeated. I gripped the cushions of the headrest and stared at my feet. "Being human is a lot of trouble," I concluded.

Silence met my declaration. I'd expected laughter. I glanced up from under my furrowed brows.

She regarded me with an amused smile. I hated that I found it attractive.

"Current, huh?"

"Don't make this worse," I begged.

"Apology accepted."

She tapped my phone against my chest. It wasn't a mink, but with her suddenly this close, the effect was the same.

I reached for the phone and my hand clasped over hers.

She took in a quick breath. In the brightness of her living room, I saw her eyes dilate. It mesmerized me.

"That body's trouble, alright," she murmured, and my head swam.

My mouth went dry, yet I felt like I was drooling. Maybe I was getting sick again. I felt too warm for the room. "Water."

"What?" she whispered. Then she blinked and shook herself. "Water. Oh, yeah. Sure."

I had to fight the urge to tighten my grip on her hand as she moved away from me. Instead, I clutched my phone with one hand and the back of the couch with the other and tried to regain control of HuVern. I should have brought a chaperone. A part of me was glad I hadn't. What was wrong with me?

Do you want to be an emu, Vern? Because this is how you become an emu.

"You sure you want water?" Kitty called from the kitchen. "I got coffee."

Caffeine sounded like a bad idea. I'd just managed to calm the coursing of my blood. "Water's fine."

She came in and handed me a glass. She had gotten herself coffee. The cup had a kitten on it, pawing at the air. The caption read, "Who's awesome? You're awesome."

"You okay?" she asked, and to my surprise, sounded genuinely concerned. Gratefully, she kept her distance.

"I don't know," I replied truthfully. "Everything gets...off-kilter...when you're near me. I don't like it."

"Yes, you do."

"Yes, I do—and I don't like that." I swallowed down the rest of the water and stared at the empty glass.

The fire crackled and popped. I loved fire. I loved the sound and the heat and the dancing light and the way it could split the clouds. But now the heat burned my hands and the light left negative imprints in my eyes if I stared at it too long. If I breathed it, I'd burn my innards. Fire was dangerous—the fire on a stove, the fire I felt around Kitty. Dragons played with fire, not humans. As a human, I loved fire. I just didn't understand it anymore.

After a semi-comfortable, charged silence, she spoke. "I'm surprised Grace let you come in alone. When's she picking you up?"

I rolled the glass between my palms. "I've not seen her in a while. She's following up a lead or trying to get me out of this cockamamie situation. I'm not sure which at the moment."

"Dang. She's that mad?"

I started to deny it, but Father's words came back to me. I shrugged.

"What's so important about this case that you turned yourself human—and like, so badly Grace can't turn you back?"

"I didn't do it to myself," I retorted irritably.

Instead of pursuing that interesting factoid like any good reporter would do, she took a cognitive left turn. She made a rude laugh. "That's a relief, because you're really bad at it."

"I am not!" I put aside memories of tripping in the shower and fever dreams of emus. It just felt good to argue with Kitty again. Normal. "If anything, I'm too good at it. I convinced you."

"Yeah. That's going to haunt me the rest of my life." She sipped her coffee.

"You and me, both. Anyway, I didn't turn myself human. Someone cursed me."

"What? Who?"

"I don't know, and we've been concentrating on trying to find Siobhan and finding a way to break the curse. I'll figure out who after that." I set the water glass on the cushion beside my phone. I pushed my butt off the edge of her couch and balanced on my own feet.

"So all that about a missing person was true?" She tilted her head with surprise.

"Of course—even the fact that she's a friend. She's a distant relative of Grace's. Why would I lie?"

"You lied about being Victor," she pointed out.

"I was undercover! It was a part."

She snorted. "A part that you've been enjoying too well. I think whoever cursed you gave you the body of an adult, but the brain of a sixteen-year-old." She pointed to her head.

I pointed to mine mockingly. "More like sixteen millennia." Never mind that Grace had said almost the same thing only a few days ago, except she'd called me 14.

Kitty rolled her eyes. "You are a girl-crazy teenager with a hyperactive pituitary gland stuck in a hot man's body."

So I was hot again? The fact that she noticed made me want to smile, which made me madder. I mean, I was gorgeous and deserved the recognition, but I needed to focus—to stay mad.

"I am not girl crazy!" I snapped.

But instead of arguing, she grinned smugly. I did not like where that grin led. Kitty didn't always come to the right conclusions, but when she did, that was the expression she wore. "Pull up a chair to the computer."

I waited until she'd sauntered out of my path before fetching a chair and rolling it to her desk.

She'd minimized whatever it was she was working on—I kicked myself now for not looking earlier; I'd only noticed she had something like 45 tabs open. As I took a seat, she accessed a folder titled with the date of the party. She paused, huffed with annoyance, and gathered her hair up, twisting it into a messy bun which she secured with a pen from her cup.

I snickered. "That's cute."

"What?" she asked; then, her brain caught up. "I work from home today. I don't bother with my appearance, okay?"

"I wasn't being sarcastic," I said defensively even as I wondered why I had felt compelled to say anything. Why was I trying to be nice to McGrue? Even so, something pushed me to try again. "Seriously. It is cute, especially how some bits escape."

I brushed back a whisp with one finger.

She turned and stared at me. "What are you doing?"

I didn't know. My brain had jammed as soon as I'd touched her. "Uhhh…"

"Believe me yet? Girl-crazy!" She punctuated her statement by poking my chest, but it felt almost playful.

Still. "You make me sound like a child."

"You're acting like one."

"Am not!"

"You make a compelling argument. Now, let me show you proof that I'm right." She spun in her chair.

She opened a subfolder entitled, "Vern???". The first photo was me winking at the coat clerk as she handed me my ticket. I didn't remember doing that.

Then came photo after photo. Me talking to Pam, leaned in close. Me dancing with Janet. And Christie. And some other woman whose name I never caught. And spinning another around then bowing over her hand… Photos of me and Cassandra. I wore that "gaze down and pout" look that Donny had taught me so well.

I swallowed. "Wow. Um…"

"Oh, you see it now?" she almost sing-songed.

I reached across her to use the mouse. I flipped through more pictures. "Yeah. I look *so good*. Definitely model material."

"That's not the point!" She tossed her head back to stare at the ceiling. The pen in her hair clicked against the back of the chair and came loose. If I hadn't been so engrossed by her photos of me, I might have tried to wind her hair in it for her. She sighed in exasperation.

But I was having fun now. "You took a lot of pictures of me. You weren't stalking me, were you? Maybe you're the one who's boy-crazy."

"Coincidence. We're losing track of the big picture, here."

"Am I? That one looks like it was taken from inside the ladies' room—yet when we crashed into each other, you acted surprised to see me. Sure you weren't lying in wait to 'casually' bump into me?"

"No." She sounded pained in her lie.

I scrolled faster. "Look. I'm questioning a waiter, so I didn't just talk to girls, did I? But you! You took..." I paused to check the bottom of the screen. "You took fifty-eight photos of me in the space of three hours. Obsess much? Victor-crazy."

"Fine!" she burst out. "I was keeping tabs on you—but not because you're..."

"The hottest guy at the party?" I teased. "You can say it. You did in the office."

She sneered at me. "Because—I thought—you were an innocent, naïve guy—"

"—who's hot."

"Naïve *hot* guy who was being taken advantage of by an uncaring conglomerate. Forgive me for not wanting to see you get chewed up and spit out."

That was actually kind of sweet—and a lot of bull. "Yes, you would. That way you could write about it."

She sighed. "Yeah, probably. But I'd have helped you get revenge that way."

That I believed, and it was sweet in a more Kitty-ish way. I relinquished control of the mouse and let her close the folder.

"Just me?" I asked.

"Of course, not just you. But you did stand out, the way that Cassandra was fawning all over you."

Ha! I knew it! She was jealous.

"Is that so surprising?" I gave her a long, direct stare with just a hint of the come-on smile that had made Donny shout, "Yes, yes! Give me more!" It was fun making Kitty squirm. Usually when I made a human squirm, it involved more teeth and threats. And drool. I could drool on command. Now it occurred to me that I could make Kitty drool instead.

She met my gaze directly for a long minute, and that electric feeling built up between us.

Then, her brows knit. "Could Fulfill the Wish have cursed you?"

I laughed in surprise. I hadn't thought of that angle. Just like Kitty to come out of left field with a theory. "To what end?"

"I don't know. To get your DNA? I saw them take a sample at the job fair."

"They wouldn't know I was going to go to the job fair. Besides, I sell my blood on the arcane market when we need to make ends meet. They can get my DNA any time they want. At any rate, this spell was not done by an amateur."

"Yeah." She swore and rubbed her forehead.

I found my gaze caught by her nails. Still painted gold from the party, they weren't long enough to qualify as claws, but I liked them, nonetheless. She ran her gilded nails through her hair. It didn't fall in luxurious waves like in the shampoo commercials, but somehow that made it all the more interesting to watch.

She caught my stare. Instead of shying away, she turned her chair to face me.

"Yeah," she repeated, only lower. "Whoever did this to you really knew what they were doing. They got the whole package."

"What do you mean?" I turned my chair to face her as well. Our knees touched. Why was that exciting? Why were *knees* exciting? But the contact had sent a jolt through me.

She didn't look at our knees. She was examining my face intently. "The flirty arrogance. The long looks. The brief touches."

She brushed back a lock of my hair. Shivers ran down my spine. My blood sang with the challenge of this game, but I couldn't help but picture an angry nun busting down Kitty's door and declaring, "Not again!"

"Maybe this isn't a good idea," I murmured, hoarsely. I reminded myself that Kitty had been playing this game most of her adult life, while I still didn't know the rules. Even so, I closed my eyes to better enjoy the sensation of her fingers playing with my hair.

"Relax," she said, not soothingly, but compellingly, nonetheless. "I'm not Cassandra. I know the limits."

Did I? I kissed her wrist and felt as much as heard her sigh. The predator/prey dichotomy was playing to my dragon as well as my human side.

"Let me tell you a story of when I was sixteen," she said.

"I'm not sixteen." I kissed her wrist again as if that made my point.

"Hush. Kitty's talking." She pressed her fingers against my lips, and I fell silent as if she'd put a compulsion spell on me. "When I was sixteen, there was this guy I was totally obsessed with."

I started to protest again, but she ran her fingers along my jawline and the stubble that was starting to soften into a beard. "He was definitely the wrong guy—forbidden fruit, you might say— but we had this crazy-wild chemistry. I could tell he felt it, too, which only made things worse. I couldn't stop thinking about him."

I was getting impatient with this story. I wanted to run. I wanted to make her stop talking. I wanted her hands in my hair. "Your point?"

"People told me to keep away from him, which only made me want to get closer. Finally, my best friend told me to get him out of my system instead."

"That worked?" I ran a thumb over her lips. It felt almost as good as her touching mine.

"Mmmhmm. Turned out half the chemistry was just curiosity."

"Curiosity killed the cat." I immediately felt stupid, tossing out Father's words like a grenade, hoping to break whatever glamour I was under. Wisdom of the Ages, and I was reduced to quipping clichés. But I was definitely curious.

Emus. You don't want to be an emu...

She leaned forward and whispered in my ear, "Satisfaction brought her back."

"I hate you." But I did not hate the tickle of her breath.

"I hate you, too." She kissed my cheek. "Let's hate each other when you're a dragon again."

"Deal."

I'd figure out the feathers later. I leaned forward as I pulled her closer.

I overbalanced in my wheeled chair. It flew out from under me. I toppled, pulling Kitty down with me. I cracked my head on the edge of her keyboard tray. The tray bounced, knocking the mouse off, which fell on Kitty's head.

"Ow!"

"Ow! HuVern, you are so bad at this!" She smashed both her hands hard against her head.

Did that help with the pain? I pressed the heel of my hand against my forehead and felt something warm and wet. I pulled my hand away and yelped. "I'm bleeding!"

"Take it easy, you big baby. It's just a cut. Come on. We'll fix you up."

She stood and offered her hand, then still holding it, led me to the bathroom. I followed, my mind reeling. Sure, I knew human skin was frail, but this was me, now. *My* skin was frail.

Was this the price humans paid for such sensitivity? When we got to the bathroom and she released my hand, I felt the motion down to my toes. Every sensation had an increased brilliance, like my nerves had been illuminated by the energy surging between us.

"I feel dazed," I said.

She turned from the medicine cabinet, a box of band-aids in her hands. "You shouldn't be concussed from a little fall like that. How many fingers am I holding up?"

She set the box behind her and held up three. I touched them with three of my own, then took hold of her hand and pulled her to me for a kiss. She stiffened in surprise, then relaxed into it. She chuckled. Did that mean I'd won or lost?

I didn't care. I was flying through an electric storm and glorying in it. I'd have to trust Kitty to know the limits.

"Band-aid," she murmured, and like a dance, she moved back to the counter as I stepped forward. With one hand, she groped behind herself for the box, pushing aside her toothbrush holder and knocking over a bottle of perfume. The aerator fell off and it spilled onto the granite.

Suddenly everything grew intense almost to the point of pain. Electricity had turned to lightning, yet all I wanted was to throw myself into the storm.

"Whoa! Tiger! Slow down."

So, I wouldn't become an emu. If I could not be a dragon, a tiger was fine.

Kitty shoved me away, laughing. "How about we take this to another room?"

I blinked, confused. That's right. We were in her bathroom. There was the shower and the toilet and the sink. The counter, with the spilled bottle of pink perfume that was making my head swim.

Then it struck me. I wasn't curious.

I'd been whammied!

I looked past her at the familiar apple-shaped bottle of Persuasion.

Chapter Thirteen:
The Power of Persuasion

I stared at the open perfume bottle in horror as whatever "Faerie/Mundane" tech gave it its reputation tried to take over my brain. The worst thing was, even knowing what was happening, a part of me was still aching to give in.

"Damsels and Knights!" I shouted and tore from the room.

I didn't stop until I was on the porch. I took in great draughts of air, in through the mouth, out through the nose, trying to expel as much of the cursed scent as I could. I filled my diaphragm like Grace taught me. The crazy, beguiling sensations that had shivered across my skin and coursed through my blood calmed, but the confusion remained, now mixed with anger. How had I not realized what was happening? They'd bragged about it in a commercial, for pity's sake!

How long had I been under the influence of that stuff? How often?

The door opened and Kitty stepped out. "Ver-er, Vic. What's going on?"

Now that I knew what to sniff for, I realized she reeked of the stuff. Yelping, I backed away fast. I hit the railing, overbalanced, and tumbled over her bushes and into the snow.

I could still smell the perfume. On my sweater! I yanked it off and threw it as far from me as I could, then wiped my hands and face in the snow.

"Have you lost your mind?" Kitty exclaimed.

I probably looked insane, sitting in the snow in my T-shirt and jeans, my face now damp with melting snow.

"Perfume!" I shouted.

She looked from me to the house. I gave her a minute to work it out. The cold was helping me, anyway.

Finally, the light shone in her mind. She smirked. "Dayam."

I threw a snowball at her. "Kitty, think! It's not funny. What are you doing with a bottle of that...witch's brew, anyway?"

"Persuasion? FTW sent it to the paper for review, and Redfeathers gave it to me."

"Well, did you have it analyzed?"

"No. We had to sign a contract saying we wouldn't. It's not unusual, apparently, but that made me suspicious."

Now, she tells me. "I could have used that information Friday night, you know. Look. Put that bottle in an air-tight container and let's get it to Grace. And get a shower!"

"Yes, fine. Come back inside. You'll catch a cold again."

Inside—in that perfume-infused temptress' lair? I laughed rudely. "I'll take my chances out here."

With a howl of frustration, she stormed back into the house. I used more clean snow to wipe my arms and neck. A moment later, she returned, my jacket held between tongs. She flung it my way.

"Phone is in the pocket. Two blocks west, there's a coffee shop—Caffeinators. I'll meet you there."

I sniffed the coat experimentally. I caught a whiff of Persuasion, but most likely just what it picked up from the ambient air. My hair probably had more from all of Kitty's fawning.

I shuddered.

I donned the coat and pulled the hat from the pocket. That would help some, and I did feel warmer almost immediately. Shoving my hands in my pockets, I headed down the street.

A thrift store stood next to the coffee shop, so I went to find a replacement for my sweater. I came across a hoodie with a dragon on it. Good—something to remind me of who I really was. And it fit.

I paid the cashier—a guy, I noted with relief. He barely looked up from his phone to make the sale.

At the coffee shop, I asked for a quiet, out-of-the way spot, and they led me to a private booth toward the back. Caffeinators had expensive coffee but reasonably priced food. I ordered a café americano and a Reuben with fries.

"You okay, hun?" the waitress asked with motherly concern.

I realized I was shaking. "Just cold. And hungry. Blood sugar's probably crashing."

I'd meant it as a joke, but she took me seriously. "Are you diabetic?"

Could I be? Wouldn't that be fun on top of everything else. "I don't think so. Just a rough morning."

"I'll put a rush on this," she promised.

I leaned against the padded booth and sighed. After a moment, I pulled out my phone.

As I had at the rectory, I got Grace's answering machine. I left a message in Faerie Gaelic: "It's Victor. I got my phone back. I'll be at the office soon. There's something wrong with the perfume Fulfill the Wish is pedaling. I'll explain when I see you. I... I miss you."

I didn't know what else to say. I didn't even know why I'd said I missed her. My head was clearing from the happy, confident, exciting fog of earlier. I felt unsettled and oddly used. Maybe that was it; I was longing for someone I could trust completely.

Where was she?

I hung up and turned my mind to the case. How did this new discovery change what I knew?

Did Siobhan discover something suspicious about the perfume? If so, she hadn't mentioned it to us. Then again, she barely knew us; Grace is distant kin—and we are detectives. She might not have wanted to make trouble for her new employer. What if she used her fancy new phone to call someone and they arranged to meet her in Cañon City or Pueblo and took her from there?

That helped the "why" and "why now" but not the "where." I pinched the bridge of my nose as I'd seen Father do at times. It seemed to help ease the growing tension along my brows.

The waitress—Adelle, I saw now on her nametag—arrived with a glass of juice and my coffee. "I don't like how pale you look, hun," she said. "You drink this right now. I don't want you passing out.

"You are an angel," I told her, touched by her kindness. "An angel of mercy."

She waited until I'd drunk half and left, assuring me my sandwich would be out soon.

Out of ideas for Siobhan, I turned to the problem of myself. Now that I recognized the perfume's effect on me, I thought back to trace the times I'd been whammied by it.

Kitty's house. No surprise there. I drank some coffee to distract myself from the fresh memories and moved on.

Kitty had certainly worn it at the party. She probably had put on more before "bumping" into me at the bathrooms. That was a sly move, and I admired her cunning as much as hated myself for not realizing it. Arrogance aside, I was not on my A-game that night. Chalk it up to the perfume.

Cassandra, of course, would have worn it at the party and the job fair. She was definitely playing me, and I had been going along like the naïve Faerie bumpkin Kitty had thought I was. That was twice Kitty's instincts were right. Had to be a record, dang it. What had awaited me in that room upstairs? How much perfume would it have taken for me to go along with it?

I flipped over the phone, suddenly needing to call Grace again.

"Waiting for someone, then?" Adelle asked. She set my plate in front of me.

"Yeah. I'm not sure when she's showing up, though."

Adelle sighed. "So glad I'm married. I'd never get used to this online dating app generation."

She left before I could correct her.

At least she was right about my needing food. I wolfed down half my sandwich and most of my fries before I slowed down enough to ponder the party more.

I was willing to bet they had pumped a low-level amount of the stuff into the air in general. That would be good for making investors feel more inclined to listen to their pitch. I realized I'd been feeling loose since I'd entered the mansion. Kind of like at Kitty's place, but more low-key.

Pam? No, I'd found Pam sweet, but not intriguing the way I'd thought Kitty and Cassandra were. Or Janet. Janet had definitely worn some. No wonder I'd enjoyed dancing with her so much.

I heard someone call Kitty's name, then a quick hushed conversation I assumed was about me. Then Kitty was sliding into the seat in front of me.

She grinned at me with sardonic amusement. "Apparently, if you are as nice as you are good-looking, I'm supposed to keep you."

I rolled my eyes. "She made assumptions. What took you so long?"

"You think I'm going out in this weather with wet hair? Besides, I had to go to the basement to find some clothes that didn't smell of Persuasion."

"Good thinking. Thanks. Hungry?"

I pushed my plate with its paltry few fries and a quarter of a sandwich at her.

She responded by holding up a bag. "I don't share food on a first date. I called ahead, and Adelle got me my usual. I paid for yours, too. Let's go. We can talk in the car."

That was also a smart idea. I doubted anyone was purposefully listening to us, but why tempt fate? Any of the fates. They didn't like me much. I wondered if they were watching me now, playing the strings of my life like a lyre—or maybe an electric guitar. There were times the past few days that I'd felt that intensity. I swallowed down the last bite of sandwich and left Adelle a fiver.

As we got to the car, Kitty said, "The perfume is in the trunk, in two baggies and an airtight container. Here." She handed me an N95 mask, still in its wrapper.

"Thanks." Even with the mask on, I cracked open the window to let the air flow.

"So were you trying to call me? Adelle said you looked nervous and kept checking your phone."

In response, I held up the phone for her to show her that her number was conspicuously absent. It did, however, hold the numbers of Grace's phone and those of her aliases. "Grace still hasn't called me back. Did you tell Adelle we're working?"

"Why bother? You may as well get used to it. As long as you're HuVern, you're going to be a hot commodity. You did apologize to Grace, right?"

Her flippant tone annoyed me. "Yes, I apologized. That's not why she's not calling."

"Well, then, why don't you know where she is?" She pulled out her sandwich and started into it, apparently expecting a long explanation.

It was a legit question that I hated the answer to. "Things got...weird between us, so I went to stay with Father Rich at Little Flower. Then I got the flu and was out of commission for a few days. Grace came to visit, but she couldn't heal me, so I pretty much slept until this morning."

"If she had a lead, wouldn't she tell you where she'd gone, or Father Rich, maybe?"

I felt marginally better. "True. So she's probably in Faerie talking to her order about this curse."

"Well, then. Where do we go from here?"

My first instinct was the police, but who knew how long it would take them to analyze the perfume, even if I-as-Victor could convince Santry that something was wrong?

I glanced at my forearm. Pam had written her phone number on it. Even though I'd washed it off, I still remembered it.

"I may know someone who can analyze the perfume for us. Head toward the college."

As she pulled out, I dialed.

"Victor!" Pam's voice reflected joy and surprise. Somehow, it made me feel guilty. "I'm so glad you called. I didn't find you again at the party, and I thought..."

She didn't tell me what she thought.

"I got sick," I said. "Just the flu, but it threw me for a loop."

"Oh, no! I'm so sorry. All better now?"

"Much, thanks. Listen, can we meet?"

Before I could continue, she burst out, "Sure! I... I mean, yeah. I just finished class for the day, and I don't work on Tuesdays—but I think I told you that?"

I got an unpleasant chill when she said, "Tuesday," but pushed my worry aside. She was nattering on about things we could do around town.

"Pam, listen. I don't want to give you the wrong impression. I need a favor. I wouldn't ask if it weren't urgent."

"Oh." I heard the heartbreak in that single word.

"It's about my friend that's missing."

"Siobhan? Well, sure then. Anything. What do you need?"

"I'll explain when we get there. Can we meet you at the Study Hall?"

The Study Hall was an off-campus café that hosted study sessions and other events in its many glassed-off rooms. I'd gamed there a few times with my friends before our group split up.

I looked at Kitty, who nodded to show she knew where it was. She mouthed, "ten minutes."

"We?" Pam repeated. That sounded more hopeless than her "oh."

I tried to cut her a break. "I can't drive. I promise, I'll explain when I see you. And you are free to refuse, just know that, okay? No obligation."

"Okay, sure. Five minutes?"

"A little longer, but not much. Get us a quiet room, please? I'd rather no one overhear us."

Now concern replaced the sadness in her voice. "That serious? You sure you don't need the police?"

"They can't help like you can. This means a lot, Pam. Thanks."

I hung up before the clever mind of hers read between the lines. Then I noticed Kitty glancing at me with amusement.

"What?"

"I think I'm with Adelle. I vote for keeping HuVern. He's much nicer than VernDrake."

"I'm always nice!" I protested.

She blew a raspberry. "You are so much nicer than VernDrake. You're flirty and attentive."

I started to protest that "flirty" was the influence of the perfume, but hadn't Grace accused me of the same thing? And that was long before I'd gone to the job fair. "I'm nice."

"HuVern gives compliments and cares about people, even little humans who don't measure up to his self-declared magnificence."

"I care!"

She ignored me. "VernDrake, meanwhile, is snarky and grumpy and thinks he's so superior."

"I'm a dragon! Of course, I'm superior—it's a definition issue!"

For some reason, that struck me as funny, and I started to chortle.

"Ha!" Kitty crowed triumphantly. "See? VernDrake would never laugh about that. He's too *mighty* and *self-important*…"

"Stop it!" But I heard the amused lilt in my voice as well as I'd heard the teasing in hers. "We hate each other, remember?"

"We agreed to hate each other after you turned into a dragon again, which is another reason to stay HuVern."

I whacked my head against the backrest. "Being human is a pain in the tail!"

"You don't have a tail. Ha!"

"Aargh! Stop it! I don't want to like you. It's weird. It upsets the order of things."

"Please! I'm a very likeable person." She sat straighter in her seat and spoke primly.

Right. Two could play this game. "Which is why your editor gave you Persuasion to test out? The perfume that's supposed to make people more attractive and likeable? Sure he wasn't putting it to a true stress test?"

"What? I... but. Oh!" She slapped the steering wheel as I laughed at her discomfiture. "Fine. I hate you!"

"I hate you, too. What'd you get arrested for, anyway? Aggravated nosiness? Tell me now."

She made a prim little snort. I didn't think she could do something so dainty. "I never said I'd tell you. I said I'd tell Victor, who is dead to me. Besides, he never earned it. Why are we going to visit some low-level lab tech from the FTW QA lab?"

"Because she's getting her master's in biochemistry and assists at the lab at See-sull."

"Aha!"

"Does that earn me the right to know about your felony?" I gave her my most beguiling grin, but she was studiously watching the traffic.

"No."

"You're mean." I crossed my arms and slouched back in the seat.

"See? VernDrake would never say that."

"That's because VernDrake is used to people treating him badly."

"And by 'badly,' you mean 'not like a superior being.'"

"Among other things, yes." My mind immediately conjured up all the times reporter Kitty McGrue had treated VernDrake badly. The teasing was getting less funny. I changed the subject. "The marketing copy said the secret was a discovery by Faerie biochemists, but I don't buy it. There are Faerie biochemists, though they don't go by that name, but in all my years among potion-makers and alchemists, I've never known anyone to successfully create, well, an aphrodisiac, for want of a better word, without the aid of magic. Let alone something that supposedly makes you better at business and making friends. All at once?"

"So they're lying? Wouldn't you know—about the magic I mean?"

We'd arrived at the Study Hall. Kitty turned into the parking lot.

I answered, "First off, not in this body. Second off, if they diluted or hid it enough, I might not immediately notice even in dragon form."

My first case in the Mundane had been an enchanted chili pepper field. I had not recognized the magic in that area at first. Although, I reminded myself, I had a lot more experience now and could better recognize when something was not right in the Mundane.

"Why are you in this form—I mean now?" Kitty asked as she put the car into park.

It was a good question that I did not have an answer to. Too many unanswered questions. About my curse. About the perfume. About Siobhan. I unbuckled my seatbelt as I grumbled. "Who knows? Maybe because I was starting to enjoy my life again."

"See? That's classic VernDrake."

We found Pam in the small study room, staring moodily at her laptop while one hand tapped a staccato on her glass of cola. She looked up in surprise as we entered.

"Miz McGrue?" Then she looked at me. "Oh, no. You are a reporter."

I sat down beside her. She did not look in the mood for a long story, and neither was I. "Not quite. I'm a private investigator."

She closed her laptop to give me her full attention. "So Siobhan really is a missing person? Yeah, I remembered. I'm good with names, and it's so pretty. Is she even a friend?"

"I met her, yes, just before she disappeared. She's supposed to have started working at FTW a week ago but never arrived. No one has seen her since she left Los Lagos."

"That's awful, but I don't know how I can help." Her expression told me she had a suspicion, though.

I plunged ahead, trying to be as vague as possible. "We have a liquid. We think it's involved in her abduction. I don't have time to take it to a commercial lab for analysis. I was hoping you could help."

"A liquid?" Her voice went flat.

Kitty opened her mouth, but I held up a hand to forestall her. "Plausible deniability. I just need the equipment and someone to run it. You can even give me the results without looking at them yourself. I'm a smart guy, remember? If I can't understand the readouts, I can find someone who can. Please, Pam. Siobhan isn't much older than you. She'd been in the Mundane all of two days when she went missing, and that was five days ago."

Her voice was small, and she looked at her knees. "You think FTW Cosmetics had something to do with it?"

"Maybe? Maybe not. Maybe it was an employee acting on his own. You're good with names. Have you heard of an Emmitt Barnaby?"

She looked out the window at the other rooms where people were studying, gaming, chatting. Living ordinary lives with ordinary demands, not being asked by a hot PI she'd just met to do something that could get her fired.

"Emmitt... Emmitt... There was a guy. I saw him once, with the big-wig PhDs when they came to visit us peons in QA. He seemed personable enough, but the animals didn't like him. It struck me as odd. They all retreated to the back of their cages when he looked their way. Remember, I told you we try to treat the animals well? I'd never seen them act like that with anyone. I never got introduced, but I remember one of the docs called him 'Mitty.' So maybe?"

She shuddered then, whether from the memory of the man or the thought that she had come so close to a potential kidnapper. She leaped to her feet and started packing her stuff.

"Do you have that liquid with you? No one will be in the labs right now."

Chapter Fourteen:
Seven Deadly Sins Shoutout:
Greed

Twenty minutes later, Pam had sweet-talked the lab director into letting her use the equipment for a special assignment she couldn't accomplish at work.

Kitty had taken my promise to heart, and before bringing in the container had taken some time to pour some of the liquid into one of the baggies. She used gloves and also washed her hands thoroughly. She gave the baggie of liquid to Pam, although she brought the whole container in case she needed more.

"Wait! Wait!" I and Kitty both yelled as Pam started to open the bag.

"The last time Victor got a whiff of that stuff, it was not pretty," Kitty said.

HuVern wanted to protest that that's not what Kitty had thought at the time, but VernDrake agreed that the whole situation was ugly, so I shut up.

Pam looked at the bag in horror. "Are you saying they *aerosolized* a...a date rape drug?"

The thought made my stomach churn. "More like a really strong aphrodisiac," I said, trying to will my cheeks not to heat up.

"But it didn't affect me," Kitty said, her hands raised in a display of innocence.

"Oh. Wow." Now, Pam was blushing, too. "Okay. So that makes sense. There'd be a different formula for guys than girls. So, okay. Why don't you go stand over there?"

I followed her pointing finger to the small alcove far from the equipment. As an added precaution, I put the mask Kitty had given me back on. The last thing I needed was another bout of girl-crazy. I had enough to worry about. Speaking of...

I checked my phone. No messages from Grace. That was starting to make my stomach hurt, too.

I texted Father.

It's Victor. Heard from Sr
Grace?

No. Choir practice at 7 tho.
She didn't say anything
about missing.

Thx

U OK?

Following a lead. Explain later.
Tell her CALL VICTOR ASAP!

I had a sudden urge to throw my phone against the wall. Grace had told Father she might go to Faerie to talk to her order. She'd told me that, too. But she also told Father she was following a lead. What if her lead was hotter than she'd thought? She didn't have anyone with her. She didn't have me.

"What's wrong?" a voice asked from behind me.

I yelped and spun. "Dams- dammit, McGrue! Don't sneak up on me." I missed my extended vision. I missed being able to swear the way a dragon would swear. I missed Grace's voice.

Dammit, woman. Call!

"Something's wrong," McGrue said. "What is it? Tell me."

I shook my head, as much to dispel the worry as to negate her words. Neither worked. Finally, I said, "Grace should have called me by now. Called someone, even to tell us she wouldn't be calling for a while."

"You're sure she's not still mad?"

"Then she'd have called Father Rich. If I just knew whether she crossed the Gap... Kitty, do you have any contacts at GSA who can check? Vern does, but I can't call them. They won't talk to me."

It took her a moment to parse what I had said. "Let me see what I can do."

She left the lab, her fingers scrolling her contacts as she walked. I watched her go, feeling useless. What could I do now? I had no idea.

But I knew what Grace would do.

I sat down, leaned over my clasped hands, and prayed.

"Ummm, Victor?"

I said a quick "To Be Continued. Amen" and opened my eyes. Pam stood beside me. "Results, already?"

"Some." She smiled crookedly. "I know it's Persuasion. Kitty left the container. The bottle was wrapped in a used sandwich wrapper."

I let my head settle onto the table and tapped it a few times. It was the best answer I could give.

She took a seat across from me. "No worries. But I need you to be honest with me, because that looked like a standard commercial sample bottle. Just how hard did this perfume hit you?"

I did not want to have this conversation, no matter what form I was in, but I trusted her. I chose VernDrake's bluntness. "Embarrassingly hard. Out-of-control hard. Had-to-flee-the-scene hard. I jumped into the snow before I did anything stupid...more stupid."

"Wow. With..." Her eyes darted to the exit.

"I don't even like her, that's how hard it hit me," I said. "I was only at her house because she took something of mine at the party and I wanted it back. She must have been bathing in the stuff."

"Wow!" She chuckled, but with surprise and a little horror rather than humor. "Okay. Thanks for your honesty. Next question—are you fully human?"

"I... I'm not sure. I may have some Magical in me." Grace had never gotten around to figuring out the specifics of my new form.

"Magical...like non-s'lem?"

I broke into a smile. I loved that she knew that word. Pam impressed me more and more, and I didn't think perfume had anything to do with it. I nodded.

"Okay. So you might have a vestigial vomeronasal organ—that's what processes pheromone scents in animals. It would make you more sensitive. That gives me some direction looking for the 'secret sauce.'"

"You are brilliant."

She shrugged. "Yeah. I'm the smart one."

I didn't like the wistfulness in her tone. I set my hand on hers. "Hey. You're not just the smart one. You're funny and compassionate and brave. And you are beautiful. I'll bet most people just see the other qualities first. Give yourself some time. You'll find the right guy."

"I was kind of hoping I had," she said.

"Me?" I forced myself not to jerk my hand away. That would wreck all the shoring up of her ego I'd just done. "Trust me, I'm more trouble than I'm worth. You caught me in a rare situation. Normally, I'm arrogant and grumpy. Ask Kitty. Plus, I drink too much. You deserve better."

VernDrake winced at that last. Like anyone deserved better than me. But...arrogant.

I couldn't tell if she believed me or not, but she pulled her hand away. "Well, thanks for being so honest. I'd better set up some more tests. It's probably going to take a few hours. I told Kitty, and she's bringing the car around. I'll call when I get the results. And... I don't care if I lose my job. If Mitty or anyone else is using this perfume to do bad things to people, then I want to know how."

"You are a rare human being, Pam Mercer. I meant every word I said to you."

As I climbed into the car, Kitty said, "My contact says he didn't see Grace's name on the records at all this week. So, your place?"

"Yes!" My urgency grew to panic. I wanted to fling myself out the door and fly. I had to remind myself at each stop sign that I didn't have wings.

To distract myself, I called Father. "When was the last time you heard from Grace?"

He didn't bother to greet me. "After Mass on Sunday when she tried to heal you. Why?"

"And she didn't leave any messages? Texts, emails, anything?"

"No, but she said she might go to Faerie." His voice started to echo my worry.

"She didn't cross the Gap."

Father swore softly. "And she never called you? I'd have thought, when you lost your phone—no messages?"

"No, nothing!" I half-yelled. Why would he even ask?

"Sorry. Stupid question. Where are you now?"

"I and Kitty are heading to my place. We've been chasing a lead."

"Kitty? Okay," Father said with a slow tone that suggested a lengthy conversation in my future. "What do you need me to do?"

I wanted to tell him to call the police and the state patrol and the FBI, but I didn't know if she was missing or where to look. What if she really was in her workshop, so caught up in whatever she was doing she didn't notice her phone had died? I'd just embarrass us. She'd be furious, too, especially when I came charging in with Kitty in tow.

Please let that be the case.

When I didn't answer right away, Father said, "Easy, Vern. She might be caught up in work. I mean, wouldn't you know if she was in trouble?"

The mizpah! I started to reach for my ankle and realized it had been days since I'd worn the chain.

"The night I showed up, I had a chain around my ankle. It had two charms on it."

"Right. I left it on the nightstand."

"It wasn't there when I woke up."

I heard him moving. "I'll bet you knocked it off when you were delirious. I'm heading over now to look. I'll call you back when I get there. Stay calm, Vern. It'll be alright."

"You don't know that." I just barely managed to keep the frantic edge out of my voice. My pulse pounded in my neck, and it was not the heady sensation I'd felt before. Human hearts beat harder than dragon hearts, I was sure of it.

He understood anyway. "Have faith, Vern. I'm praying."

I waited until I hung up to snarl. Faith! What I needed right now were wings and enhanced senses and my fire!

"Breathe, Vern," Kitty urged. "Slowly or you'll hyperventilate, and that won't help Grace."

"Right. Right." I forced myself to think about my breathing. Fear-filled adrenaline coursed through my body, screaming for me to do something. The panic that gripped me proved as encompassing as anything I'd felt with Kitty and was even harder to fight.

"It'll be alright," Kitty soothed. She reached out and rubbed my shoulder. The touch made me want to crawl out of my skin. Why hadn't I gone straight home?

"Just drive," I snapped.

She jerked her hand away. "Fine! Jeez! Don't take this out on me. It's not my fault."

"Yes, it is! It's your fault and mine and that stupid perfume and this goddamn curse."

"Whoa! Okay. You're right. It's all our faults, but getting mad isn't helping anything. Not that kind of mad, anyway. You need to access that inner VernDrake."

I agreed, but I didn't know how. HuVern seethed with guilt and fury. I looked out the window and counted down the blocks until we got to my lair. Just a few more minutes...

The phone rang.

"I found it." Father's voice now rang with worry. "The mizpah is charred and there's a hole burned into the carpet where it was lying."

I didn't take God's name in vain this time, but I swore a very human swear word.

"Vern, calm down. You can't help Grace like that," Father said.

We'd pulled up to my place. Kitty hadn't even put the car into park before I'd tumbled out and was bounding up the steps. I fumbled for the keys and was shouting Grace's name as soon as I'd opened the door.

Silence and cold greeted me.

"Vern?" Father said over the phone.

I hung up and called Grace's number, praying to hear her ringtone in the building. Nothing.

I dashed to the office and grabbed my real phone. My hands shook as I tapped in the code to find her phone.

Nothing came up.

I tapped out the spell Grace had put on the SIM card. Still nothing.

"No!" I howled. I swore, every profanity I knew, human and dragon. She was gone, just like Siobhan, and for who knew how many days, and all because I had been stupid and selfish and a sensualist and...

A snowball smacked me in the head.

I spun and found Kitty in the doorway.

"Get a grip, Vern!" she yelled. "I don't care how worried you are. A temper tantrum isn't going to help Sister Grace. Now calm down or so help me..."

She held up another snowball threateningly.

"But it's my fault!" I wailed. Then, as if all my energy had escaped through those words, I sank into a chair. I buried my face in my hands. My shoulders shook.

"It's my fault. I should have listened to her. She told me to stay home. Then I'd have been here for her. Instead, I was off having fun playing Victor and she was on her own and—hey!"

Kitty had poured snow in my hoodie then pulled it over my head.

"Jeez! Enough already," she scolded. "You are so much drama! There's plenty of blame to go around. I sent her the coat-check list which could be the lead that got her into trouble. And for that matter, she didn't tell anyone where she was going. No backup, really?"

"Don't put this on her!"

"Then don't put it all on yourself. Or on me, for that matter. Are you ready to actually address the problem, Vern? Or should I get more snow?"

The snow had started to melt down my back. It gave me the willies. I did my best to brush it out of the hood and my hair. I took off my jacket and shook out my hoodie. My dragon hoodie, which I'd bought to remind me what and who I was.

I shook myself hard, imagining myself shaking out my tail and snapping my wings. It grounded me.

"Okay. I'm better."

"You sure? I can get more snowballs."

"Ha, ha. Go in the kitchen and see if she left a note." I opened the computer to check for the same and to see if she had a file with clues she'd discovered. I found Kitty's email unopened.

"She never opened your email," I shouted.

"At least it wasn't my fault, then! But she was still mad at me?"

"It's not always about you, McGrue." I usually checked emails in the mornings. That meant she might have left on her lead without checking and never come back. Kitty's email was dated 10:45 a.m. Monday. One email from Father, from about 10:15, had been opened, but nothing after that. I scrolled down, swallowing down panic like bile, letting my anger rise up instead.

Someone had my nun and was going to pay.

"No note," Kitty reported as she joined me in the office.

"And she hadn't checked our email since early Monday," I added tightly.

Kitty clamped her lips tight, probably afraid expressing her concern would set me off again. It was too late for that. HuVern had had his tantrum. VernDrake was back and out for blood.

"No out-of-office message, either," I added.

"That means she expected to come back, then, right?"

I caught her implication. "Which means she didn't think what she was doing was going to be risky."

Kitty snapped her fingers. "You know, we didn't even think about the ordinary. She might have gotten into a car accident. It's not like they could have gotten a hold of you."

Someone would have called Father. Still, we had to follow the lead. Who knew? She could be in the hospital with amnesia—how was that for a cliché? I told Kitty to start making calls while I went to check the living area of our lair.

I'd already noted in my mad dash to the door that our car was missing. In her room, I found the phone and keys gone, too. The spell hadn't located her phone. That meant more than the phone was out of juice. The SIM card was destroyed or so far out of range that the magic could not reach it. That meant outside the US and most of Canada and south of Central America...

I squashed the thought. No. More likely, they'd destroyed the SIM card. That would break the spell. Occam's razor.

What other clues?

I checked her closet. Her snow boots were tucked neatly in their place, but her heavy-duty hiking boots were gone.

I dashed down the stairs, hollering for Kitty to check the kitchen drawer for missing flashlights. She called out acknowledgment, but I heard her still talking to a hospital, asking about Jane Does, then to be transferred to the morgue. I forced that thought and all the others that followed out of my head and ran to her workshop.

Jackpot.

We had built Grace a separate room inside the warehouse we called home. Her workshop housed an odd combination of Faerie and Mundane contraptions, with bottles marked "eye of newt" (actually a flower and not a lizard) and "dragon's blood" (actually mine), next to Bunsen burners and a small centrifuge. Pam would love it.

What drew my eye, however, was the large map of Colorado taped to the whiteboard. Small cards with identifiers clustered around spots throughout the south-central part of the state. The side counter was littered with bags bearing matching IDs. They held assorted items—hair, plastic cups, lipstick-stained napkins.

I felt a surge of pride. While I'd been bumbling about as HuVern, my crafty nun had been collecting DNA samples of all the guests for a tracking spell. I started doing a quick count, trying to determine how long it would take her to complete such a complex undertaking.

"Good news/bad news," Kitty called as she walked in. "No sign of Grace in hospitals from here to Pueblo. Whoa. What is that?"

"Tracking spell of the partygoers. She must have cast it late Monday morning."

I went to the map and started ticking off locations as Kitty took a photo. "That's the FTW Colorado Springs corporate headquarters. That's the airport. That one...probably the lab where Pam works."

"That's the Chieftain or nearby," Kitty said, pointing to a spot in Pueblo. "Could be the city council building, too. They're trying to get Fulfill the Wish Cosmetics to build in Pueblo."

"She's looking for where they might be holding Siobhan—if they are holding Siobhan.

It's not going to be in a crowded building, most likely. Nor residential."

"Why not? Plenty of kidnappers have basements."

"It's not that kind of abduction," I said. "Besides, Grace is wearing hiking boots. That means rural or farmland."

"It would help if we knew why Siobhan was taken," Kitty complained.

Just then, Victor's phone rang.

Pam sounded worried as she greeted me. "Didn't you say Siobhan was part Magical? Was she siren by any chance?"

I swallowed hard and forced my voice to stay calm. "Yeah. Why?"

"Okay. This is really sus, but the secret sauce to Persuasion? Almost entirely siren pheromones."

My world tilted. I staggered and braced myself against a counter. Dimly, I heard Kitty call my name.

"Vic? Does that help?" Pam asked.

My heart threatened to beat its way out my throat. "More than you know," I rasped. I cleared my throat and tried again. "Good work, Pam. You may have saved two lives."

"Two? Oh, wow—that's why supplies are limited, isn't it? Oh, wow. Ohwowowow..."

Her rising distress activated my protective instincts, and I felt myself calm and focus. "Pam. It's okay. Listen carefully. Here's what I need you to do. Download all that information into a thumb drive. Remove any identifying factors, like the university logo or time stamps. Wipe your fingerprints off it. Put it in an envelope and address it to DragonEye, PI, and drop it into a random public mailbox. No return address. Then erase everything from the university computers. Not just trash it. Make sure the files are wiped. Can you do that?"

"Oh, wow. That's cloak-and-dagger. Am I in danger?"

I prayed not. "I just want to keep you from losing your job."

"Aw, you're so sweet. But I don't care, not if..."

My body ached with the urge to get moving. "Pam, I've got to go. Remember: random public mailbox, no return address. Delete the files."

"Got it. Good luck."

I hung up and pressed my fist against my forehead. *You will not panic, HuVern.*

"What's wrong?" Kitty asked.

"They're using Siobhan for her siren pheromones. And now they've got Grace."

Chapter Fifteen:
Not Love, Actually

"Come again?" Kitty asked.

"Their pheromones! They're both siren/human crossbreeds. Fulfill the Wish is milking them for their pheromones to put in Persuasion." Despite my best efforts, the fear was rising in me again. Why did humans have to feel so strongly? No wonder so many ran when they saw me.

I wanted to run. I needed to fly. I braced my hands against my knees and tensed my back as if I could will myself to grow wings.

Meanwhile, Kitty was saying, "They're doing what? Oh, that's disgusting! But I got my bottle before Siobhan went missing."

"That only means she's not the first victim." A muscle spasmed in my back, but I didn't feel any wings sprouting from my skin. Dagnabit. But at least the exercise had calmed my nerves, somehow. I stood and regarded the map, the piles of party trash, the neat rows of potions and charms Grace created for us. I didn't have wings, but I had tools. My partner had made sure of that.

"You'd think something like that would make the news," Kitty said sarcastically.

"Maybe it has," I said. "It's not like the victims would show signs of foul play."

Kitty started tapping on her phone. In the meantime, I pulled out the small square box of drawers Grace had gotten from the hardware store. In each drawer were charms she had been creating for use during cases or for protection. After our case with the Lance of Longinus, we'd made it a priority to stock up. I'd eaten nothing but rats and roadkill for a month so we could put my grocery money toward supplies. Now, that sacrifice would pay off. Once I figured out where we were going, I wanted to have everything we needed.

One thin drawer held St. Anthony charms, charged but not activated. I scanned the area for something of Grace's I could attune them to. Next, I gathered others—healing, shielding. Most zapped me when I tried to touch them. Whoever cursed me into this form didn't want to make things easy on me.

"I found two," Kitty announced. "One in November, a prostitute found dead north of Colorado Springs. They said she was too far from the Gap for too long. The other was in the mountains, mid-July. Cause of death—exposure and dehydration."

"That makes sense. They'd pull the pheromones from sweat, urine, or oil in the hair."

"But pheromones are pretty specific. They wouldn't need to...?"

"Don't think that!" I snapped. I was already worried enough about what they might be doing to my innocent nun. "Look. Siren pheromones are different. They're like...like the stem cell of pheromones. Sirens can consciously manipulate them. Legends always talk about sailors being drawn by their singing, but song is the catalyst. If the biochemists found another way to trigger them..."

"Or maybe they're just enhancing human pheromones!" Kitty exclaimed. "That would explain why Persuasion is supposed to help you be more successful in career as well as romance. It changes based on what the woman wants."

"Exactly," I said, although I was reassuring myself rather than agreeing. There were plenty of ways to make Grace sweat without hurting her physically or emotionally. I told myself they were limiting themselves to just that.

Kitty went to the map. "The 'hiker' was found around here." She traced a circle west of one of the spots Grace had pegged.

I pointed to the site. "That's where we're going. Can you get us there?"

"Sure. I have four-wheel drive and hiking boots in my trunk. I can get us close."

I was suddenly thankful for the hiking boots Father had found for me. "Good. Come here."

I handed her six chains.

"What are these for?"

"We're going in armed."

She snorted. "I'm from Philly. I'm always packing."

I filed that interesting tidbit for later. "Magically armed, McGrue."

I pointed at the drawers of charms I'd pulled out, naming the spells: healing, shielding from magic, protection from physical assault. I directed her to load five chains with several, then the sixth with the ones that had not zapped my fingers. It was significantly fewer, and Kitty commented on it worriedly.

"I'll make do. Here." I handed her the last two St. Anthony charms. "These are set to find Grace. Put one on one of the chains. You'll wear that one. Then put the other one on mine."

Once done, I had her hold the chains in her cupped hands.

"Now what?"

"Pray."

"I'm not sure I believe."

I snorted. Figured. "No atheists in foxholes."

I knew an activation spell—as a dragon. No way I could mimic the purrs and clicks I needed. Would Grace's song work for me?

What choice did I have? I prayed and then sang.

Kitty gasped as the medallions flared. "I didn't know you could do that!"

"Thank God I can. Now, put that one on, and keep two to put on Sister Grace and Siobhan if you find them first. Give me the other two." She did as told and dropped the other two into my jacket pocket. I slipped the other one with the fewest charms around my head.

"Let's go," I started for the door, but she grabbed my arm.

"Look. You know me. I'm all about the story, and I'm not afraid to take risks when pursuing a scoop. I'm with you, okay? But maybe in this case, we should call for backup?"

I glanced at the map. It was still in the county.

"I'll call on the way," I promised as I pushed past her to the exit. My body was screaming for action, and each step toward rescuing Grace was a relief.

Kitty followed.

While she put the coordinates into her GPS, I called my friend, Sheriff Bert.

"I need your help. Grace is in trouble."

"Who is this? Where's Vern, and why are you using his phone?"

Drat. I'd forgotten my voice had changed. "It's me, Vern. Long story short, I'm in human form.

But you once asked me for relationship advice about Natura, and I told you unless you were wearing armor, I didn't have anything to suggest."

There was an insufferable pause. Then, "Alright. I believe you. But how the heck...?"

"Long story! Do you have anyone near Old Silvermine Road? Just south of West Antelope Mountain?"

"That's just south of the county line."

Why was he not answering my questions? "I know where it is! Do you have anyone nearby?"

"Vern, chill," Kitty urged.

"Who's that?" Bert asked.

"Kitty McGrue, and she's going to be the only one helping me rescue Grace unless you catch up! Please, Bert. Grace was following a lead and I've not heard from her in two days, and I think someone around there has captured her. We need your help—and no more stupid questions!"

There was a pause in which I imagined Bert biting off the plethora of questions threatening to escape from under his cheesy mustache. Then I heard him holler to Dispatch to get some cars heading to Old Silvermine and that he'd update them in a minute.

"Alright. I have people on the way. But I need clearer directions and a lot more details, so we know what to expect. Talk."

"It'll take us twenty-five minutes to get there," Kitty assured me.

As briefly and with as little embarrassment or self-recrimination as possible, I explained the situation: the curse, Siobhan, the other part-siren victims, and finally how I and Kitty were on the way, armed to the teeth with magical items to find and rescue Grace and any other Faeries that FTW might be holding hostage to its "Faerie/Mundane technical innovation."

As I spoke, I heard the scrape of his chair and his footsteps as he left the office. At one point, he made me pause while he transferred me to the car's speaker.

"We're probably looking for a little side road off Old Silvermine," he told me. I could hear the sirens wailing in the background.

"Tell your guys to come in quiet," I urged. "We don't want anyone to know we're coming. It's not snowed up there since Sunday, and Grace traced them on Monday. There should be tracks where they pulled off."

"Plus, Grace's car," Kitty said loudly enough to be heard over my phone.

"I hear ya. Now you two listen to me. Don't go in alone. Find the place, park out of sight, and wait for us. Closest deputy is about ten minutes behind you."

"Not a chance," I said.

"Vern, if you are human, you are vulnerable. It's a whole lot different getting shot as a human than as a dragon."

"It's no picnic getting shot as a dragon," I retorted, although I was suddenly aware of the lack of protection charms I was wearing.

I grumbled. "We'll be careful, but I'm not waiting around."

"You said she's been gone for days," Bert argued. "Ten minutes isn't likely to make a big difference for her, but it could mean a huge advantage for you, both for your safety and your success."

Fighting Bert was a waste of energy. "Fine, but hurry."

I hung up before he could reply. We'd left the city. Spruce and pines flashed past on both sides of the highway. I couldn't fly. I couldn't scent her. I couldn't even tear the upholstery in frustration.

I did the only thing I could.

I prayed.

"Vern? We're close. Keep an eye out on your side."

I said an "amen" and opened my eyes, turning my attention ahead and down, where the road met the woods. Kitty had slowed down—a good idea in this winding, snow-and-ice-packed one-laner, anyway. I strained to catch a glimpse of a break in the trees. I gripped my St. Anthony medallion, the better to feel the smallest change that might signal that Grace was nearby.

"How sensitive is Grace's spell?" Kitty asked.

"Maybe a mile or two. Wait! There!"

Kitty slowed so I could snap a photo of the turnoff to send to Bert. I wasn't sure it would help because the area looked like any other area.

Kitty, however, stopped just after turning off, then gunned the engine while her left foot smashed the brake. I heard clumps of dirt smacking the back of her SUV.

"It's murder on the brake pads," she said as she put the car into four-wheel drive, "but hopefully, the deputies will see it."

"Smart." I texted the information to Bert as she started up the road that was little more than a couple of ruts in the thick snow.

"Learned from an old boyfriend."

"He needed to mark his trail?"

"No. He was just an idiot. Hey, is that a...parking lot?"

A moment later, we'd pulled up to a small clearing. A van and a car were parked side by side.

"That's not Grace's car," Kitty noted.

"No. But they could have moved it." If I weren't so worried about Grace, I'd have been annoyed. We'd just paid that hunk of junk off and gotten it new snow tires. "Come on."

I got out and started searching for footprints or a hint of a trail. I started to feel a tug on my chain and turned to tell Kitty.

She, however, had made a beeline for her trunk. She pulled out a backpack and a camera.

I gaped at her and waved my hands askance. Grace was in utter peril and Kitty was thinking about her article?

But she shoved the backpack at me. She tucked her hair into her hat and wrapped a scarf around her neck. "Cover story. We're a couple of hikers."

I reined in my temper. Once again, she had thought of something I missed. "Okay, but in the middle of winter?"

"It's a beautiful afternoon. We took a long drive, saw the side road, and on a whim decided to go on a short hike. Look—other people had the same idea, right? Their cars are right there. Now smile, Honey."

She took my photo before I could comply.

I peeked in the backpack. Winter survival supplies. Probably for the car, but good for our story. I donned it, and we set off where St. Anthony led.

There wasn't a trail branching out of the parking lot, and I didn't see any footprints. Someone had covered their tracks well. Since I didn't have my dragon senses to rely on, I'd have to trust St. Anthony. I held the medal out in front of me, and we followed the minute changes in its swing. We weren't close yet. Once or twice we mistook a normal motion for a clue and had to backtrack.

Kitty checked our position on a phone app, but we'd lost cell service before we'd gotten to the parking lot. She made occasional marks on the trees—I guessed that was the Girl Scout in her, not the felon—and took photos.

After about a quarter of a mile, we came upon a "deer trail." The medal pointed straight down its path. I tucked it into my hoodie, and we started down the trail. It was peacefully silent, only a disinterested bird here and there and the rustle of a rabbit scurrying from our presence. On another day, HuVern might have enjoyed it.

We'd hiked in silence for about 15 minutes, when Kitty stopped and rested her back against a tree. She'd tucked her camera sideways so it rested on her hip.

"Honey," Kitty said warmly. "C'mere."

When I got near, she grabbed my coat and pulled me into an embrace.

"Go with it," she hissed before I could react. "One of my medallions is acting up."

Fewmets. I put my arms around her back. "Cold, hot, or tingle?"

"Cold."

"Someone's watching us. Could be a surveillance camera. We need to get off the trail, backtrack if necessary."

"Let's make it convincing, or someone watching might suspect. Follow my lead and don't take it personally."

She kissed me.

VernDrake was not happy at the development, but HuVern remembered all the moves. We were pretty convincing.

Then she let out a throaty giggle, took my hand, and pulled me into the forest where the trees were thicker. We went a couple of hundred feet, occasionally stopping for a kiss for our possible audience's viewing. Finally, she dropped my hand.

"Ok. It's back to normal. That's really handy. Can I keep it when we're done?"

"No. Let's try again but approaching at an angle away from the trail. Hold the medallion and stop at the slightest change in temperature."

I pulled out my phone. Still no service. I looked at Kitty.

"Me, neither, but the trail app works. Want to go back and wait for the cavalry instead?"

Bert had said they were ten minutes behind us. Or rather the nearest deputy was. Would he then wait for the others? Had they seen the turnoff? The sensible side of me said we should go back, but my skin was crawling with a new urgency. What if someone had been watching the trail and didn't buy our hiking lovers act?

What if Bert and his deputies found the trail and crossed into the surveilled area? Would that put the kidnappers on alert or distract them and allow us to get in?

As quiet as the woods were, we would have heard anyone coming up the trail. We had a few minutes. I chose a compromise. "Let's try to recon the place, then head back and catch them on the trail."

We wove a careful zigzag in the direction of the trail, trying to follow St. Anthony and the warnings of Kitty's charm at the same time. Soon, we found ourselves at the edge of the woods looking down into a cleared area with a small, utilitarian building.

We ducked down behind a conveniently thick growth of small evergreens. Kitty pulled out her camera. I noticed now that the lens had a hood on it to keep from reflecting the sunlight. I hoped it helped against light bouncing up from the snow.

She took photos. I squinted, trying to get details of the doors and guards. How did humans manage with such limited eyesight?

Then Kitty nudged me and passed me the camera. Oh.

Through the telephoto lens, I counted two doors in sight, a couple of moving cameras, and a single security guard that stamped his feet and was probably questioning his career choice. I felt a predatory grin steal across my face. Maybe I could help him with that.

No. I promised Bert I'd wait. He'd been in the army before becoming sheriff. He probably had a better idea than just rushing the guard and hoping for the best.

I scanned the area more widely, taking note of other features. No fences; that was good. I saw the back fender of a jacked-up SUV. There must be a road somewhere. Good to know in case Siobhan or Grace were not able to run.

I didn't want to think about that.

I took some photos, then tapped Kitty on the shoulder. We backed more deeply into the forest.

"Does your criminal record include hot-wiring cars?" I asked.

She snickered. "I saw that car, too. We're going in with backup, remember? Still, that building is just a shack. Which means..."

"There's probably a bunker underneath it," I finished. "There are cameras on every corner of that shack. There might be some kind of motion sensors in the snow, an electric fence or something. We won't be able to sneak up on them."

"So we find the road, go in sirens blazing."

"Who knows what they'll do to Grace if we do that. Not good."

Kitty was looking at her phone. "It gets worse. We're on the other side of the county line."

"Fewmets!" I managed to hiss and not yell. That was worse than worse. Outside his county, Bert's hands were tied, especially with only my hearsay to make him suspect any wrongdoing. He'd have to call his counterpart and arrange a co-op. Maybe he could find a way to convince him and let us all go ahead, anyway, but even if he did, that would take time.

Time we didn't have if someone had seen us on the trail. Even if they bought our reason for traipsing off and seeking privacy in the woods, they'd probably send someone to check on us or our car.

"What do we do?" Kitty asked.

I thought fast, as VernDrake and HuVern. "Give me your gun."

"Pardon?"

"Give me your gun. I'm going to find a way in there. In the meantime, you go back, find Bert, and tell him I went rogue, took your gun, and went in alone looking for blood. That will give him the excuse he needs to cross county lines."

She tutted. "And meanwhile, you'll be all alone? Against who-knows-how-many armed guards?"

"I'll sneak in. I have a stealth charm. If they're all as attentive as Frosty out there, it won't even be a challenge. Besides, if it's underground, there's probably a vent or escape hatch. That's my way in."

She laughed rudely. "Did you read that in *Better Evil Lairs and Gardens?*"

I ignored her. I pulled out the St. Anthony medallion from one of the two chains she'd given me—enduring the reflexive zaps from the other charms. These, I'd attuned for escape. Now, I quietly sang the activation song while praying for an ingress. Almost immediately, it swung to the right.

We followed, Kitty gripping the early warning medallion once again. A few minutes later, we were at a large circle that had been covered with snow and cut branches.

I smirked at Kitty. "I think it was *Villainous Architectural Digest*. They didn't even bother with a camera here."

I started clearing the area around the cover. Kitty watched worriedly.

"What if there are some cameras inside? They might not care if someone sees the manhole, but if someone goes in, that's a whole different story. They could shoot you on the ladder."

I held up the St. Dismas medallion. Thankfully, that one didn't care that someone had cursed me human. "Stealth spell, remember? It only lasts twenty minutes or until I'm noticed, but as long as I can get in, I can get down the ladder."

"And if the cover is alarmed?"

I pulled out a device that I legally should not own. I was all about making the most of Faerie and Mundane tech in my business. "Unless it's a particularly high-end alarm, this will take care of it. Now give me your gun and go find Bert."

"And leave you alone? Hell, no." She planted her fists on her hips stubbornly.

"Kitty. This isn't some story you're after."

"No, it's *the* story. Pulitzer, for sure."

I knew she was putting on a brave act. "It's dangerous."

"Exactly why you need backup. Besides, do you even know how to use a gun? We're wasting time. How long do you need to check for an alarm?"

I gave up. Arguing with Kitty had always been a waste of time, and it was starting to get dark. "A couple of minutes."

"I'll be right back. Don't leave without me."

I watched her traipse purposefully into the woods. With a sigh and shake of my head, I started working on the portal cover. By the time she'd returned, I'd deactivated the alarm and worked open the heavy door.

"What did you do?" I asked.

"Set my trail app to a lost hiker alert. It's a pretty specific frequency and short range, but the sheriff's walkie-talkies should pick it up. I left a text for Bert on the phone. Then I made a fake trail before backtracking my steps and coming back here. I was a terror as a Girl Scout."

I didn't know if I should be surprised or impressed. "I'm sure you were."

She smiled prettily. "Thank you, Honey."

HuVern grinned back, but I quickly turned serious. "Are you sure you want to do this? You aren't immortal."

"Are you sure you are?"

I didn't have an answer. "Grace is my partner. My responsibility."

"You think I want to spend the rest of my life plagued by guilt if something happens to either of you while I stayed up here like a coward? Now activate the spells and let's go."

She started toward the ladder, but I shoved ahead. "Age and beauty first," I quipped.

I was already descending before she could do more than tut indignantly. Good. If, by some chance, the stealth spell didn't work, I would be the one they shot at first. I didn't want to spend my unending life plagued by guilt, after all.

Chapter Sixteen:
Seven Deadly Sins Shoutout:
Wrath

Five minutes into the stealth spells later, we were down the ladder and looking at a long, clinical hall, blessedly empty. Kitty moved to mark the wall, but I stopped her. I held up the St. Anthony medallion. It swung toward the shaft. She nodded to show she understood. We'd be able to find our way back.

Using the one tuned for Grace, we took a left. The villainous architects apparently decided they didn't need cameras in every hallway, either. We must read the same magazines. Nonetheless, we were careful to duck under windows, even the frosted glass ones on the office doors. Kitty had stowed her camera in the backpack, which she carried so I would be free to pounce on any guards. However, she occasionally paused to snap a quick shot with her phone, exposing only the top of the phone as far as the lens and clicking blindly.

I used mine in a similar way to peek around corners.

"This place is awfully empty," she murmured, looking at the latest photo. "And weirdly prepped."

I responded with a nod. So far, we'd passed a stable, a human-sized aquarium, and rows of huge planters. Lab equipment, too. Quite a lot of it was still under plastic, but a few looked disturbingly used. I made a point to scour the records for missing persons on both sides of the Gap for Magical/human crossbreeds.

We were coming to a junction when we heard footsteps.

I lunged back, planting my back against the wall. Kitty did the same. We traded glances. She reached behind her, where I assumed she had her holster. The footsteps were light, not like combat boots that I'd seen on Nanook, Guard of the North.

I held up a finger. Wait.

As the lab tech strolled past, I sprung out of our hall and grabbed him, clamping one hand over his mouth and the other around his waist.

Oops. *Her* waist.

She was feisty, too. She struggled and tried to smack me with her tablet, but I'd immobilized her arms at the elbows. Her face mask kept her from biting me, but she did try to smash my nose with the back of her skull. I leaned back, lifting her bodily as she tried to kick my shins. Fortunately, she wore pretty little ballet slippers. Gloria's toddler kicks had been more painful.

Kitty hissed and pointed to a janitor's closet she'd opened. Not bothering to argue about the cliché, I carried in my wriggling prey. Unable to hit me, she tried to smack Kitty with her tablet. Kitty grabbed it away.

Normally, I like prey that's a challenge, but right now, this one was more trouble than it was worth. I may not know a lot about being human, but I did know human anatomy. I switched my grip to her neck and pressed against her carotid artery until I felt her slump against me.

"Holy crap, Vern!" Kitty managed to let her horror show even though she whispered. "That was dark."

"You'd rather shoot her? Hey—that's Cassandra!"

The mask had slipped from my victim's face. Even so, I hardly recognized her without the low-cut silk clothes and fancy makeup. Not to mention the lack of perfume.

Kitty chuckled even as she found a roll of duct tape. "You have a way with women."

"Aw, thank you, Honey." I paused to bat my eyelashes at her before searching Cassandra's pockets. I snapped the SIM card on her phone—poetic justice—but other than her lipstick, she didn't have anything else on her. I pulled the lanyard with its keycard off from around her neck with a yank that lifted her shoulders off the floor.

"A little miffed, are we?" Kitty asked as she pulled a long stipe of tape.

"She led me on!"

"And you followed like a puppy on a leash." Kitty said as she taped Cassandra's mouth, then her hands and feet. She wasn't exactly being gentle, herself.

"That's not the point."

Kitty snorted as she started on the knees, elbows and fingers. I nodded, impressed. Someone understood the power of leverage.

"Girl Scouts?"

She met my smirk with one of her own. "We were a tough troop in Philadelphia. But see? I told you this one was trouble. She was going to kidnap you!"

"That's not what you thought she was going to do with me. Besides, that had been part of the plan. If she'd kidnapped me from the party, Grace would have used our charms to follow me."

"...and then you'd both be kidnapped?"

"Shut up."

I grabbed the tablet. It hadn't gone to sleep mode yet. Too excited about being used as a blunt weapon, I supposed. I pulled up the report she'd been studying. It was mostly gobbledygook, but I did see two sets of measurements attached to a single room number. The measurements were taken an hour ago.

"They're alive." For a moment, I felt weak with relief.

We had no way to lock the closet, so we tucked Cassandra back in a corner.

"How's that for feral?" I asked her sleeping form as Kitty stuffed the tablet into her backpack. "No one messes with my nun."

"Feeling better?" Kitty asked as we snuck out of the closet.

"Not until we have Grace and Siobhan, no."

Our stealth charms were useless now, so we opted for careful speed as we headed the way Cassandra had come, following the St. Anthony medallion and the room numbers. Sure enough, the charm about yanked the chain off my neck as we neared the room on Cassandra's chart. It was at the end of the hall; I almost toppled head over heels from the insistent pull. I swiped Cassandra's key, and Kitty went in first, gun out like she was in a cop show.

The room was ablaze with light and enough heat to make me homesick for my old lair nestled in Mt. Vesuvius. Two hospital beds were occupied. If I hadn't known whom to expect, I would not have been able to tell if they held men or women. They were encased in heavy, voluminous rubber suits and skullcaps. Tubes came out the backs, dripping liquid into a container. IVs fed into the arms of both.

Someone was standing beside one, about to inject something into the IV.

Kitty jerked the gun in his direction. "Freeze!"

He turned in surprise. His name tag said, "Barnaby."

Emmitt.

A red fog washed over my vision. Human or dragon, I knew what that meant—and I didn't need any persuasion to act on my impulse.

I crossed the room in three long strides, my fists clenching along the way. As soon as I was in swinging distance, I clocked him on the jaw with everything I had.

He fell like a sack of bricks.

Unfortunately, my hand screamed as if I'd hit a sack of bricks.

Ow!

I clenched my teeth and shook out my hand, my body buckling over in pain and my foot stomping even though I'd not told it to. Nobody ever mentioned that hitting someone hurt!

"Vern!" Kitty called me to the present.

Alarms were going off. Kitty was helping the person near her sit up. The girl was rag-doll weak. Siobhan.

I looked at the woman on the bed in front of me. Grace stared at me with desperate, terrified eyes.

"Grace!"

I clawed at the straps holding her down and ripped off the tubes attaching her to the equipment. My hand screamed in protest. I didn't care. I could hear the bootsteps pounding in the corridor. We'd seriously underestimated security.

I gently pulled out the IV with my good hand, then hastened to undo the knot of the ball gag they'd shoved in her mouth. But I could not remove the shock collar around her neck.

Grace sat up and took a huge breath.

"*Ah-a-ah AH!*" she sang, and the notes echoed off the walls.

Her collar shorted out and splintered, pieces disintegrating as they fell from her neck. The tanks shriveled and melted. Equipment around us burst into sparks and flames. The heavy door went flying off its hinges, and we heard shouts of pain and gunfire as it sped down the hall. Then more gunfire and painful shouts. Guns clattered to the ground.

Retreating footsteps.

Grace gulped air like a drowning woman. Then she buried her head into my shoulder and let out sobs that were half screams.

"Grace! It's okay." I hugged her tight.

"Vern!" Kitty hissed. She was already pulling Siobhan to her feet.

"Just wait!" I snapped. Kitty didn't understand. Grace had been held prisoner for months by the powers of Hell as they tried to twist her voice to their purposes. Now someone was leeching her power from her very body. She had to be reliving every nightmare of her hellish imprisonment. Her current captors might not be demons, but they were evil, nonetheless.

I pulled off the offensive skull cap and stroked her sweat-soaked hair. "Shh. It's okay. I'm here. It'll be alright."

"Vern!" Kitty called. She'd found a wheelchair and had settled Siobhan into it. "They'll be coming back! We have to go."

"Right! Okay!" I fumbled in my jacket pocket. My hand encountered my knit cap, and I put it on Grace's head, muttering reassurances the whole time. Then I set both of my extra chains over her head. Immediately, charms started glowing. Through it all, she clung to me and sobbed.

I grasped her shoulders and pushed her away from me so she could see my face. "It's going to be okay. I'm getting you out of here. We have to go. You can do this, Grace. Ready?"

Clearly, she was anything but. Nonetheless, she swung her feet off the bed. I had to catch her as her knees buckled.

"If you can't run, I'll drape you over my shoulder, and that will be awkward for both of us."

Maybe my tease worked, or maybe the charms were taking effect. She stood straighter. Leaning on me, we raced out the door, Kitty and Siobhan not far ahead. Kitty was dodging debris while Siobhan giggled almost drunkenly. I cradled Grace's head against my shoulder, shielding her from the sight as we ran down the hallway littered with broken masonry, injured guards, and melted guns.

"Don't look. Don't look." I told her. We'd deal with the aftermath of her spell later. Who knows? Maybe she could go heal all the guards after Bert arrested them.

"I'll never hear 'Immigrant Song' the same way again," Kitty called back to us.

Despite myself, I laughed. It had taken me a year to convince Grace to watch the *Shrek* movies with me.

As we ran, I activated Grace's charm to find the nearest and hopefully safest escape. Miraculously, we made it to the elevator without any encounters. Even better, the door opened right away. We ducked into its relative safety and punched the button for the top floor. For a moment, we could catch our breaths.

Elevator music played a muzak version of "My Chemical Romance."

I and Kitty avoided each other's gazes.

"They might be waiting for us at the top floor," Kitty warned. She tried to move Siobhan's wheelchair closer to the wall beside the door, out of the line of fire.

"Who?" Siobhan gasped. "How?"

"We'll explain later," I told her. I glanced at the numbers. Seven floors to go. "Just be ready to run when we say."

She gave me a goofy smile. "You are so handsome."

I turned my face away quickly. I hoped it was just heat exhaustion making her delirious. I did not need to get whammied by an actual siren half-breed swimming in her own sweat. Not that I was giving her much notice. Grace clung to me as if she thought I'd vanish if she let go. Now that we were standing still, she'd buried her head against my shoulder again, too. I ached with the desire to protect her, and that worried me.

"Grace? That doctor. What was he...? What was in that...?" I didn't want to voice my suspicions.

She shook her head. "Just a sedative. I put up a fight."

Siobhan giggled. "She chewed through two gags and almost got us out once. She was amazing."

Pride and relief washed over me. "Told you." I softly sang, "Amazing Grace, how fierce you are," which earned me a weak snicker. Good.

Three floors to go. I pulled Grace's hands from my jacket, met Kitty's eyes, and jerked my chin toward Siobhan. "Give me the backpack and get ready."

I smacked the second-floor button just before we got to it.

As the doors opened, I tossed out the backpack. When that didn't get shot up or cause anyone to run screaming thinking it was a bomb, we took hold of our charges and ran. On her way out, Kitty smacked the button for the bottom floor. Smart. Hopefully, that would buy us some time.

I scooped up the backpack without breaking stride. I kind of impressed myself.

Kitty yanked it from my hands. "You'd better not have broken my camera."

"Buy a new one with your Pulitzer," I retorted.

The staircase led us to the parking lot. We paused at the door. I heard shouts in the distance. They'd discovered our ruse. The mountainside was dark. Maybe they wouldn't see us until after we'd stolen their car. Hopefully, Kitty could hotwire it.

As soon as we stepped out, motion-activated floodlamps filled the area with light.

Figured.

At least the car was close, and the doors unlocked. Siobhan was able to climb into the back seat by herself, so Kitty ran to the driver's side, did a brief search for keys, then started pulling wires from under the dashboard. Grace kept missing the high running board. With an apology, I scooped her up and settled her in. The exertion had taken more out of her than the charms could replace. She tilted, and if I hadn't been there, would have fallen out.

In the background, however, I was hearing shouts: *Freeze! Sheriff's office! Drop your weapons!*

I laughed as I grabbed the seat belt and pulled it to fasten her in. "Hear that? The cavalry is here at last. We're almost there. Just a few more minutes, and—"

A shot, like the crack of lightning, split the air.

Something poked me in the back.

A plink, and a bullet bounced off the metal buckle of the seatbelt.

After it had gone through my chest.

I stared stupidly at the red stain growing on my jacket. "Oh. Uh..."

Then my legs wouldn't hold me any longer.

Grace screamed.

I did not remember hitting the ground. I was vaguely aware of screams and another gunshot and fluffy white snowflakes, so bright in the floodlights. But it all seemed distant, almost surreal.

Then Kitty was pressing her scarf against my chest and shouting for help, and Grace had my head in her lap and sang healing spells that bounced off me. Why would they do that? There was a big hole in my chest. You'd think that would be an easy entry point.

Then came pain and a bizarre alternating wooziness and knifing that matched the throbbing of my heart.

"Ow," I murmured experimentally. The word did not fit the experience. I coughed and tasted blood. I grimaced. That wasn't fair. As a dragon, I liked blood.

"Shh." Grace soothed, though her voice shook, and her tears mingled with the snow on my face. "Just stay still. It'll be okay. I'm right here. Just concentrate on my voice. It'll be okay. You'll be alright."

I didn't feel right at all, but I was glad she was there. Would she stay while I hibernated? I felt like this one was going to take a while. Lots of healing sleep. Sounded nice. Others were coming. I thought I heard Bert. That was good. He'd help her get me back to the lair.

Kitty was talking too, something about hanging on and her Pulitzer and my face. "So don't you dare die on us, do you hear?"

Oh. I was still human. Humans died. Was I dying?

I must have asked because Grace started shaking. "No. No, you silly dragon. You can't die. You can't!"

Her sob slit the air like the shot that split my heart.

"Don't cry." It was hard to talk. Things were getting blurry. My eyelids drooped, but I forced them open. I wanted to see the snow. I wanted to look at Grace. I needed her to know I was there. That I'd always be there. My limbs felt heavy, like wet sacks of sand. I forced my arm up, anyway. I meant to wipe her tears, but I think my hand just flopped against her face.

She pressed my palm against her cheek.

"You're not dying," she said. "You're a dragon. You'll outlive us all. You'll live through the millennia."

A bit of song drifted into my consciousness, like a snowflake. *Through millennia and more*. It was a good song. Very dragony.

"I love you through the millennia and then I'll love you more," I sang, but my diaphragm wouldn't cooperate. I couldn't get my breath for the next verse. It didn't matter.

"I love you, Grace."

I meant it as VernDrake and HuVern.

Her lips trembled. "I love you, too."

She leaned down and kissed my forehead.

That was the last thing I knew.

Chapter Seventeen:
True Love's True Form

I came to in a strange kind of awareness. I was aware of *me*, but not my body, human or dragon. A blazing, glorious, yet comfortable brightness surrounded me. Peace infused me, yet at the same time, I could not help wondering.

"That's it? I'm dead?"

"Well," replied the familiar voice of St. George, "that all depends."

He appeared before me, his armor resplendent, the crimson of his cloak so vibrant it might have hurt to look at its perfection if perfection were not the norm here. His body bore no scars—disappointing, because I'd personally given him some beauties. His hair, cut in the pageboy style no one had liked at the time except him, suited his face perfectly. I could have just stayed there, admiring him and the skill of the One who created such magnificence.

He grinned, and that was perfect, too. "As usual, you have made trouble, my dear friend."

I waited. I didn't know if I raised my brows like a human or tilted my head like a dragon, but the intention was the same.

"You were shot," he explained, "through the heart, or at least through the left ventricle."

Listen to him, being all medical.

"Yeah. I was there. Sounds pretty fatal in a human," I replied, bemused. I felt a lazy contentment about it all.

"It would have been except for your unique situation. You were cursed into your human form, after all. Do you remember what happened at the end?"

"I told Grace I loved her, and she said she loved me."

A sudden warmth of joy spread over me. How I could feel anything more vibrantly than what I was already surrounded by, I didn't know. And yet, this memory, this knowledge, burst from me like its own kind of song, but one that was felt by the entire soul.

"And then?"

"And then she kissed me." And somehow, I was even happier. I felt like I was shining brighter than a star.

George grinned at me like I was especially cute in my realization. "Exactly. True Love's First Kiss. The guaranteed curse breaker for any spell."

My shiny happiness dimmed with confusion. "But she kissed me on the forehead, and I didn't get to kiss her back."

George shrugged. "It doesn't make it any less true."

I hadn't thought of that. "Huh."

"Since True Love's First Kiss broke the spell right at the time of your death, you are in a unique kind of limbo. You have a choice."

"Die a human or live a dragon?" An hour ago, that decision would have been a no-brainer. Now, however, I wasn't sure I wanted to let go of this peace. If I didn't feel so perfectly adored, I'd be jealous of the mortal races.

"It's a little more complicated than that." George smiled at me like a father about to give his son the greatest gift of his life.

"You have been a good and faithful servant, Vurnerrah. You've endured much and accomplished great works, perhaps more than you realize. But there is much left to do. So you shall return to the living, but you may choose how you wish to return—as a human or a dragon. With all your wounds healed, of course."

"But what about Grace?" I asked. I felt like I should be upset about this offer. Grace was a nun, after all. If I returned as a human, it'd be awkward and unfair for both of us. She'd have to leave, or I would. But we'd still love each other every day of our lives—that's what True Love meant. I wouldn't do that to her, not even for the chance of returning here someday.

"What about Grace?" George asked.

"If I went back human..."

"You think she'd forsake her vows for you?" he arched an eyebrow.

Oh! As human, I'd still be able to do that, too! "Well, True Love? And it is me."

He crossed his arms and looked at his shoes, shaking his head. His hair fell over his face so I could not tell if he was frustrated or laughing. I did feel a gentle impression of both around me, like I was a child who had done something both exasperating and endearing.

Finally, he said, "Are you sure that ego will fit through Heaven's Gate?"

I shrugged. "At heart, I will always be a dragon. Besides, God can do anything."

Besides, if my choice meant I had to flee Grace or risk ruining her, I didn't really have a choice, and it was rather unfair to offer it.

It was the first snarky thought I'd had since dying, but somehow, I didn't feel judged for it. Instead, I felt comfort, as if all had been considered, and I was commended for considering it myself.

George replied, "You may overestimate yourself – or underestimate Sister Grace. However, she, like all sapients, was given the gift of free will. You have only to choose for yourself and then respect her choice."

"Of course."

"Then you may decide. For True Love's First Kiss, you shall take True Love's True Form."

"You're paraphrasing *Shrek*." I felt a lazy, perfect amusement at that fact.

He shrugged. "I may have watched it with you a time or two."

"You're wearing Charming's haircut."

He rolled his eyes. "I wore it first. No more stalling. Decide."

"Can Grace become a dragon?"

Now I felt amusement all around, reflecting back at me. Was this how it felt when angels smiled at you?

George said, "This is your transformation, Vurnerrah. Not hers."

Too bad. She'd have made an amazing dragon.

Surrounded by love and acceptance, I thought about it. All I'd wanted since I woke up human was to be a dragon again. To have my tail back. To fly. To breathe fire and sense magic.

I would never die. Maybe I'd never return to this peace, but I'd be with Grace for the rest of her life. And someday, some glorious day, my kin would return, and we'd dance and fill the sky with wonder again. People would look upon us with awe and through that awe remember the magnificence of God.

I'd never see my kin again as a human, most likely. Even if I did, I'd never dance with them.

But to be human. To taste scrambled eggs and feel the patter of the shower. To sing in the choir and laugh until tears came out of my eyes. To sit so close to Grace our noses almost touched and stare deeply into her green, green eyes. To sing melody to her harmony.

Would I ever get to kiss her? What would it be like to kiss someone, as a human, and have it really mean something?

Still, as a dragon, I could protect her better, and hadn't I found contentment curling myself around her and sheltering her under my wings? And how wonderful it felt when she rubbed behind my cheek crests or caressed the soft spot behind my horns. I'd loved her before I became human. I'd love her afterward, too. I'd love her for a millennium and a thousand years more. A dragon's love was legendary.

Still, to live as a human knowing someday, I'd return here...

Both were choices with blessings beyond measure—but who was I kidding? There was only one real thing to consider.

I told George, "I appreciate being given the choice. Truly, I do. But only one thing matters. In what form can I best serve God? That's the form I choose."

"Even if it means never having a romantic relationship with Grace?"

"Obviously. God's will, not mine."

I felt a sudden exaltation around me.

George laughed. "Excellent. Return then, my friend, and be blessed. You are indeed wise."

"Of course, I am," I said as the brilliance faded. "Don't sound so surprised."

Snow fell into my open eyes.

Even so, I could not make out the individual shapes, just a cottony, white blurriness masking my vision. I couldn't blink them away. I couldn't make my lids move at all.

Everything around me had frozen. Even my lungs had stopped. They weighed heavy in my chest. Blood still seeped from my back but now as a lazy ooze. Sticky, too.

People around me were yelling. Kitty kept repeating, "Don't you dare die on me!"

For all the good her caterwauling would do.

Grace's lips were still on my forehead but moving in prayer. I wished I could tell her what her kiss had meant for me—for us—but my mouth wouldn't work. Someone draped a blanket over her. That was thoughtful. Wish someone would think to do something about my eyes.

Then a large, thick-fingered hand covered them and eased the lids shut.

I heard a pain-filled keening.

Don't cry, Grace. Patience, my silly nun.

A moment later, I felt myself lifted, floating, enveloped in a brilliant light that glowed yellow and white through my closed lids. For a moment, I thought God had changed His mind, and I was going to be assumed into Heaven like Elijah. A fitting way for a dragon to go, if I had a say.

But no, I was returning to life.

I felt no pain, but a curious feeling of expansion, as if every cell in my body suddenly learned to breathe from its diaphragm. My heart healed, grew, changed. My hands and feet elongated, and the nails thickened and hardened into proper claws. My eyes shifted apart as my entire facial structure altered.

My neck stretched and stretched and oh, how good it felt as my vertebrae popped and multiplied from the base of my skull to the prehensile tip of my tail. My tail had returned! Yes! Even better, my shoulder blades rotated ninety degrees and nubs burst from my back and unfolded into wings.

All this time, my insides rearranged, missing organs grew back, my skin hardened into scales. My bones reformed into cheek crests, horns, and spikes.

I opened my frost-lashed eyelids and beams shone from my eyes. Magic flared from every part of my body, so pure and brilliant, even the Mundanes saw it and gasped. Then it collapsed back into me.

I had returned!

Still in the air, but holding myself aloft, I took in a deep breath through the dragon equivalent of the diaphragm, reared my head back, and let forth a white-hot flame into the sky. It seared a hole in the clouds and lit the ground brighter than the day. The song it sang was of unbridled joy and gratitude.

Then I laughed with complete abandon as I did a loop in the air. I was back! I was healed. I was me!

I looked down to share my joy with my human companions. Many had ducked for cover—a fitting response. Bert waved his hat and cheered. Kitty alternated between sniffling and clapping. Grace...

Grace was still kneeling on the ground, the blanket around her like a shroud. She stared up at me with a mix of love and awe and frailty.

I dove and swooped myself around her just before she collapsed.

"Vurnerrah."

"I'm here. I'll always be here."

I butted my head against her shoulder and sheltered her with my wings.

Chapter Eighteen:
Seven Deadly Sins Shoutout:
Gluttony and Sloth

Two days later, Grace and Siobhan were recovering in the hospital, paid for courtesy of a very frightened cosmetics company. I had had time to nap and think, not only about the case but the curse, which was why I was ready when I saw the demon sitting on the roof opposite the warehouse.

I snagged the bottle I'd bought the day before and flew up to join Acediadeus on the roof.

"What are you doing watching my home?" I demanded with a long-suffering tone.

"Hoping to see rishathra?" Acediadeus quipped, using the word Mundane science fiction author Larry Niven used for interspecies mating. It was regaining popularity now that there were actual intelligent non-humans to mate with.

"Like that's ever going to happen. Don't be gross," I chided. I handed him the brown paper bag. "Here."

He opened it and regarded the label with suspicion. "This is the good stuff. Like actual, quality hooch."

I settled down on the edge of the roof so I could swing my tail off the side while we talked. Acediadeus and I went way back —all the way to the Great War where we'd been pitted against each other like spy vs spy. I'd hoped the last time we'd met, I'd gotten rid of him for good, but I realized yesterday that he'd just been biding his time. I'd not given him enough credit, but I would not make that mistake again.

But first, I had to figure out how he'd managed to curse me in the first place.

Hence, the bottle of scotch. The only way Acediadeus got to drink was if someone willingly gave him a drink, knowing what he was. Naturally, he had no willpower and very loose lips once the alcohol hit his system. I wondered if His Demonic Nefariousness had arranged that. If so, I hope he never figured out what a miscalculation he'd made.

"Well, everything turned out okay. We saved Siobhan and stopped an evil cosmetics company from harvesting Magicals for ingredients. I have a greater appreciation for humanity. Grace and I are closer than ever. And we got paid. All in all, a good day for us, so I figured you deserved something."

"Hold on. You're saying this is a consolation prize?"

I shrugged. "Consolation prize. Tender mercy. However you want to call it."

He snorted. "Consolation prize, then."

Acediadeus unscrewed the cap and drank half the bottle before slowing down. So predictable. I liked when he made things easy for me.

"How'd you know it was me that cursed you?" he asked when he came up for air.

"Process of elimination. There were so many ways someone could curse me, including making me human. But why make me sexy? I mean, sure, it's a natural conclusion that I'd be attractive in any form, but *crazy-hot?*"

"Self-depreciation is not a good look on you," Acediadeus sneered.

"I'm serious. I'm gorgeous in any form. There's no getting around that. But I'm a dragon. I don't mate. I don't have a mating drive. That would take a lot of tinkering, and I haven't ticked off anyone with that much power so badly that they'd want to take that kind of time and energy. Or that would want to be so creative about it. Then I thought of you."

I grinned at him affectionately. It was pure sarcasm, of course. We'd been at odds since our Great War, when I'd bested him for possession of the Lance of Longinus. Specifically, I tracked him down like a rabid bloodhound, swiped the thing out of his hands, and ate it. I felt rather proud of it at the time; then, the physical and spiritual indigestion hit. When I came across the Mundane version, I played it smarter and burned it to a crisp instead.

At any rate, I'd been sick and depressed for a century before coming to the Mundane, and who did I find but my archenemy, exiled to this universe by the Prince of Darkness himself. We crossed paths now and then as he tried to earn his way back into Satan's good graces. I knew his weaknesses, and he thought he knew mine.

Acediadeus raised the bottle in acknowledgment of what he took as praise. "It was no small feat getting past that stubborn dragon mindset. I jacked up your hormones so high I don't know why you weren't crawling out of your skin when you even saw a pretty lady, much less when they threw themselves at you."

Come to think of it, about 90 percent of the people I met on this case were women, and they all wanted to get close. "Did you arrange that, too?" I kept my tone admiring to keep him talking.

"Nah. It wasn't the intention, anyway, but it was in the spell."

"Pheromones, then. You jacked those up? You sly imp. No wonder Cassandra was sniffing me."

Acediadeus smiled lasciviously. "She was something."

"True." Should I mention to Acediadeus that he had made it easier for me to get my foot in the door at FTW? "She must have had a sensitivity of some kind. And she was on the hunt. At some point, at the party or later, she'd have kidnapped me and milked me for my pheromones, too."

He laughed. "Can you imagine the chaos that would have caused in the world? Such a missed opportunity. I wish I'd thought of it. I could have tweaked things just a bit. That would have been a good *consolation prize* if we couldn't bag that nun of yours."

Grace? Now, that answered a lot of questions.

Grace and I were best friends. We knew each other's secrets. She'd come down to comfort me when I had nightmares, just as I would ascend the stairs to comfort her against hers. She'd been so hesitant, even scared, for me to get outside help with the curse, almost like someone had built an aversion to that thought. Or maybe jealousy about someone else saving me? Her fear that I take the sacraments. If I'd listened, it would have left me spiritually weaker and less able to fight the spell. (And let's face it, I'd had problems as it was, especially when Persuasion got involved.)

As if reading my thoughts, he muttered, "Stupid perfume threw a wrench in the plans. You have no idea how hard I worked to make adjustments."

So he hadn't expected me to get whammied?

Grace was part siren. Maybe I hadn't had a vestigial vomeronasal organ. Maybe I'd been sensitive to the perfume because I was sensitive to her.

I could sing. Beautifully. And she'd loved it.

I wasn't the victim of this spell.

I was the weapon.

And Fathers Rich and Stone and the bishop had all seen it. I should have known better than to disregard the instincts of consecrated men.

"Did you really think you could engineer the fall of Grace?" I asked, as if I'd known all along.

It wasn't a great pun, but he winced, nonetheless. Puns—the pinpricks to a demon's soul.

He gurgled down more of his "quality hooch" and belched. "It might have worked, too, if you'd been a good little human and stuck close to the person you trusted most. A little more time together, a chance for her to try to save you, consoling each other like you always do. It would have worked! I'm sure it would have worked. But no, you thought it was fun. You wanted to explore your humanity at a party."

He snickered. "In that car though! She was so jealous, and you were right there! Just a nudge and it would have been over —the whole *Phantom Menace* Anakin/Padme romance."

"Look at you, with your Star Wars references!"

"But no! You had to get all chivalrous."

"Love does that."

"Love." He snorted rudely. "That, and hanging around too many priests and knights. Oh, but the reporter babe! Mmm-mm. I thought I had you, then. The perfect way to trap you in your human form and start a love triangle, too. I could have worked with the jealousy. It might have taken longer, but I'd have ruined all three of you. I could have worked with jealousy. Yeah, I could have..." He muttered assurances, almost lulling himself into a stupor.

Then he jerked upright with a start. "But you had to go spill out of your chair!"

"Yeah, such unlucky timing for you." I'd thought back over that morning, however, now that I was in my right—a.k.a., dragon—mind, and I firmly believed that our chairs had had a little angelic assistance when they rolled out from under us.

The thought of having victory snatched out from under him had energized Acediadeus. His voice rose in volume and he started swinging his arms. "I was furious! Satan was furious! I had to beg for another shot. I licked His Darkness's clawed toes, and he'd been stepping in the brimstone!"

"TMI."

But he wasn't listening. "I almost had you during that rescue. Satan's children, you were so freaking heroic and protective. Never mind the rescue itself! You shielded her eyes, so she didn't see the people she'd hurt? That was next-level. Covering her hair, putting her seatbelt on..."

"I'm thoughtful like that," I preened.

He paused to take a swig. "And that was all to my favor, it was. I was set. All I needed to do was make her too afraid to go to the hospital. You'd have taken her home, carried her to bed, maybe sung that million-years song... I could see it all in my head. It would have been disgustingly romantic until I got my way." He started kissing the bottle with increasing suggestiveness.

I tried not to gag. "Shall I leave you two alone?"

His pantomime ended in a curse. "Why'd you have to get shot?"

"Aw, should you have been protecting me instead of daydreaming about my demise?" My tone was snide, but inside, I was shaking. Was that shot just random luck? Or had it been the only way to stop us from a soul-damaging mistake? Acediadeus had calmed to hugging his bottle and was swaying a little and chuckling to himself. Time for the most important thing I needed to know.

"Speaking of protection, I have to congratulate you on getting past Grace's shields," I said. "That was exceptional work."

He burped. "Shields! Ha! I'm not getting through those unless I get a personal invitation. She's that freaking good. No. I set that spell up on you months ago, when you were visiting her in the hospital."

I hid my relief with an eyeroll. "After I destroyed the Mundane Lance of Longinus? Acediadeus, are you ever going to get past that?"

He waved the bottle about vaguely. Did demons get hangovers? I'd bet Satan arranged it so Acediadeus did, regardless. "It was a brilliant plan. Brilliant. The spell was set to go off when you and Grace had reached a critical point in your friendship."

"Aw, you big romantic, you." I hoped Satan was listening. I could only imagine how embarrassed he was at this moment.

Acediadeus replied with a belch that came from his diaphragm.

I stood and stretched. "All's well that ends well—at least for Grace and me. How much trouble are you in?"

"Nothing I can't handle." He peered one-eyed into the bottle as if wondering where it had all gone.

"Isn't that Hubristous' line? Leave us alone, Acediadeus. You aren't going to win, especially now. You've only made us stronger."

With that, I took off. I had some errands to run before I visited Grace.

Later that afternoon, I landed on Kitty's front porch. I was surprised at how much trepidation I felt. Confronting a demon had been easier, and all I was doing for her was dropping off a gift. It wasn't like I had any residual feelings for McGrue...

No, wait. I did. Embarrassment. Humiliation. A sneaking suspicion that, if I were honest with myself, I'd think the experience had been fun. No one could ever know that.

Yeah, definitely humiliation.

Snow had fallen the night before, and I was glad not to see the evidence of my earlier spill off her stoop. This was going to be hard enough without me being reminded of our last encounter. I settled myself into a regal pose in front of the doorbell camera and rang it with my tail.

"What do you want?" Kitty demanded from the speaker. She was taking the going back to hating VernDrake seriously.

I held up a thumb drive to the camera. "Piece of your Pulitzer, courtesy of an anonymous source."

The door opened, and Kitty all but snatched it out of my claws. Did she think I was going to pull it away? That was her game.

She asked hungrily, "The formula? For Persuasion?"

"Plus a few other interesting facts no one else in the press knows about. A thank you for helping me save Grace's life."

"She okay?"

Kitty rolled the thumb drive between her fingers and didn't look at me. Rude.

"She and Siobhan should make a full recovery, but the doctors are keeping them a few more days just in case. I'm heading to the hospital next."

"Good to hear." Kitty started to shut the door.

I stopped it with one large paw. "What? That's it?"

"Were you expecting an invitation in?" She curled her lip at me. She also positioned herself to block the doorway. What did she think I was going to do, push my way past? It's not like she had my cell phone hostage.

"No!"

"'Cause I've fumigated the house and had it cleaned professionally."

"I know. I could smell the disinfectant halfway down the block."

"I'm not into inter-species stuff." Her eyes flashed.

What was wrong with her? "Gross, McGrue!"

"Then what?" she yelled.

Kitty had reached a new level of ingratitude, and the fact that I didn't know why only annoyed me further. "What do you mean, 'what'? I let you in on the scoop of the decade, and I don't even get a thank-you? It's not like I'm expecting you to tell me how you got a felony or anything. Although..."

She tutted indignantly. "I should thank Pam, not you. Besides, it was my scoop, and I was already investigating."

I tossed my head in response. "Please. You didn't give Pam a second thought. Admit it. You'd have gotten it all wrong without my help."

"Your help?" She opened the door wider, presumably to have more room for yelling. "Who needed help saving Grace? And wasn't it me who was trying to hold your guts together while you were declaring your love for her?"

"Guts? I got shot in the heart. There weren't any guts."

She flung her arms in exasperation. "I know! I was there. Anyone else would have just died, but not you! No, you had to have a long, dramatic death. I was trying to keep you from spewing blood all over everyone while you serenaded Grace and declared your undying love. You want to talk gross?"

"Did you want me to sing for you?"

She ignored the jab. "Nobody sings after being shot through the heart! But it always has to be about you, doesn't it? Even as a man, you were drama. Then you float in the air and get all glowy and turn back into a dragon, like, like that scene from *Shrek*. Well, just so you know, I am not writing that part. You get enough attention as it is."

"Wait—you think I died for the *attention?*"

"On top of all that, I ruined a perfectly good scarf trying to keep you from bleeding out, thank you very much."

I decided to end the fight while I was ahead. "Finally! An expression of gratitude. You're welcome."

Her mouth moved wordlessly for a few moments. Then, she let out an inarticulate howl and slammed the door in my face.

I stared at it, bemused, unsure whether I should still be angry or laugh at the absurdity of it all. Irrational. She'd completely lost it. Grace would not be happy with my report, but at least I'd delivered the information. I'd have to count that as a win.

As I turned to go, my wonderful, amazing, oh-so-appreciated dragon hearing picked up McGrue from behind the door.

"It was a BLM rally in Philly. I was supposed to be reporting and got carried away."

"Typical," I said just loud enough for her to hear. I could have been referring to our earlier conversation and not commenting on how she'd gotten a felony on her record. I'd never tell.

I launched myself off the porch.

Four legs and a long body meant stairs were a hassle again. Fortunately, the Los Lagos General Hospital had elevators.

Grace and Siobhan shared a semi-private room on the third floor, courtesy of FTW Cosmetics Corporate, who was claiming they did not know about the "unauthorized illegal and unconscionable activities" of its "Faerie/Mundane" tech team. At least, they were willing to help prosecute the people involved (in other words, throw them under the bus), and they were footing the bill plus some compensation for emotional damages.

The sheriffs had also rescued a small pack of werewolves, who had been told that FTW was going to help them find a cure for their affliction. Guess when Marketing said that Pelt would bring out your inner wolf, they weren't kidding. They would be finding out what it meant to deal with wolves if the pack decided to sue.

But for now, everyone had been rescued, and Grace and Siobhan were recovering. That's what mattered to me.

I could smell the flowers in their room even as I exited the elevator. People had sent Grace so many cards and bouquets, I'd suggested we start a florist shop. Instead, she'd insisted Father take the nicer ones to the church. That was my nun.

I had something better to give her.

"What's this?" Grace asked as I plopped a velvet bag onto her lap. She opened it to find one of her St. Michael medallions

"You are never to leave the lair without one of these," I told her. "I already have two in my internal pouch. You're going to take some of the money FTW's giving us to make a whole slew of these. We always have a backup."

She slipped it over her head, but regarded me curiously, nonetheless. "Is there a particular reason?"

"I'll explain after you feel better. Until then, just trust me and wear it always?" I gave her an entreating look.

She blanched.

"What?"

"Nothing," she said, but when I tilted my head encouragingly (how I wished I still had eyebrows), she said, "It's just, well, you had the same kind of expression as a human. It took me by surprise."

"I had a bunch of my grins, too, although my threatening ones weren't nearly as effective."

"Oh, they were effective, but not how you intended." She shivered.

"There was a reason for that, too—which I promise to explain once you are home and fully recovered. Let's just say I was not the only person getting whammied and leave it at that. I saw McGrue today. That went about as good as could be expected."

As I had hoped, my change of subject made her chuckle. "I daresay she was whammied as well."

"Well, she's over it. I almost took back the thumb drive."

"Thumb drive?"

"Mmm-hmm." With my fabulous peripheral vision, I made sure no one was walking past who might overhear me as well as took in Siobhan and the room. I liked this room. It was free of the invasion of medical monitors that I'd seen in the FTW lab—and the last time Grace was in the hospital.

I continued, circumspect nonetheless. "An anonymous source sent it to us—postmarked Canon City." I had to credit Pam for that detail. She was a smart cookie for a Mundane. "It's the last nail in the coffin for FTW Cosmetics. A chemical analysis of Persuasion that proves they were harvesting siren pheromones for their current production. I'm taking another copy to the D.A. I think he's going to owe us some favors. As is our due."

"It's not just about us, Vurnerrah," Grace chided.

I replied amiably. "Of course not. It's about justice for you and Siobhan and Rolfran and his pack. Us getting a bennie is icing on the cake. How is she?"

I jerked my head toward Siobhan, who lay sleeping in the other bed, her back to us and the covers pulled high over her head.

Grace regarded her kin sadly. "She had a difficult night. In addition to the trauma, the detox is hard."

"Rough."

"I don't think she'll stay in the Mundane, but it doesn't matter. As long as she recovers."

"She's got the best helper ever for the process right here. What about you? You're sure they didn't...?"

I must have sounded worried. She reached out to caress between my horns. "I'm fine. They only kept me sedated. They wanted me sleeping and sweating. They didn't dare try anything else."

"You're too dangerous awake. Kind of dragony that way."

Her eyes flashed like a dragon's flame. "I'd have chewed through that ball gag if you hadn't rescued me first."

I thought about her *Shrek 2* Snow White scene. "I have no doubt. You are fierce and determined."

Suddenly, though, she didn't look so determined. "I should have never gone off alone. And I should have stayed closer to you. Not just because I put myself in danger. I didn't realize how overwhelmed you'd gotten."

"I think you were overwhelmed, too," I pointed out. "All things considered, us being apart was probably for the best."

"It was so strange. I'd never felt like that before about anyone. You were still my dragon, the person I laugh with, confide in. Chastise when needed. I don't think I've ever told you how grateful I am for what you've done for me this past year and a half. I've loved being a team. I thought we could face anything together. But when you turned human, I was terrified. You were so beautiful!"

"I don't understand why everyone keeps acting so surprised about that," I grumbled good-naturedly. I settled my head in her lap, doglike, so she could scratch better. Nothing in the human experience compared to getting rubbed behind the cheek crests.

"Don't joke about this." Her voice was quiet. "I came so close to forsaking my vows for you— human you. Only my fear of what it might do to the spell stopped me. How could I ask you to stop being a dragon?"

I was beginning to realize there was no end to how deeply I could love someone. I leaned into her hand. She responded by digging in a little harder with her knuckles. How I missed getting my cheeks rubbed!

"First, thank you. Second, I think you're underestimating the power of your convictions. That curse was meant to affect you as much as me."

She sighed. "Which you'll explain later?"

"Just keep Saint Michael near you." After a moment, I said, "And let's just agree never to let it happen again, okay? It was horrifying. I mean, you left me to the not-so-tender mercies of Kitty McGrue, Pulitzer Prize Hound. I still shudder."

Her fingers paused and tensed for a moment before continuing their mission. I remembered the unopened email from Kitty. Now, I had to wonder if the title ("What Vern and I were doing last night") might have contributed to it being left unopened. You'd think a reporter would have a better understanding of how to write a headline.

However, Grace said kindly, "She might get it this time. That was an exceptionally good article in today's paper, especially considering the state she was in when we were helivacked out. I'm glad you gave her a copy of the information, but how in the world did you two partner up?"

I felt an edge in her seemingly innocent question. I answered with bland reassurance.

"I went to retrieve my phone which she'd taken from my coat at the party. Then we were sharing information and realized the perfume had caused all the trouble, which meant you were in trouble. She refused to let HuVern go haring off on his own. Besides, she wanted a story, and I needed a ride."

I vowed to tell her the rest when she was recovered...or in a year or two, when it got funny. If it could ever get funny.

But Grace didn't want to let me off so easily. "A story? That's it? Some common concern and the desire for a story? Because as I think back, she was pretty upset that you were shot."

"More people should get that upset when I'm shot. Besides, I ruined her scarf."

"Aye, true," she mused, humoring me as she scratched a soft spot at the base of my horn.

I closed my eyes drowsily. For the first time in a long time, I wished I were smaller. Then I could curl myself up by her side like a service animal. Her own personal emotional support dragon.

"At least dying broke the curse," Grace said.

"That wasn't dying," I murmured. "That was True Love."

Grace laid her head back against the pillows with a contented sigh. "Ah. Aye. I suspected it was."

Do you love Vern?

Please take a few minutes to leave a review. Don't know what to say? Share what you loved – or hated – about Vern's transformation. It helps readers and helps with Amazon ratings which makes author and dragon happy.

Acknowledgements

I've had this story in my head since before I wrote *Live and Let Fly*, which puts it somewhere around 2010, I think. Unfortunately, the only part of the plot I knew clearly was the Vern/Kitty bad romance, which was not enough to do anything with. So, like many great ideas, it got set aside until the characters gave me more.

After *Nun of My Business*, I had a much stronger idea of the Vern/Grace dynamic and the story started playing in my mind again. I thought I could do a short story...if I could find a mystery to tie it together. Sarah Crickard, a great friend and another wonderful writer who is in my CWG SFF crit group, encouraged me to use the perfume idea as the mystery and then add the human/Faerie trafficking. That nudge made the mystery explode, and a short story turned into a novel that I cranked out in a month. Thanks, Sarah!

It's so fun to have people that will play with you. Thanks to Rebecca Martin, Matthew Schmidt, Lisa Harmon, and Cesar Chacon, who helped me brainstorm some of the sillier aspects of FTW Cosmetics products and advertising. Also to all the people at the Catholic Writers Conference Live who gave me a bunch of ideas of how a dragon may be confused by the human form.

I'm a big fan of Jane Lebak's writing and am tickled to say she's a fan of mine. We often talk about our stories, and she has some of the best ideas ever. Thank her for Vern forgetting he doesn't have wings every time he trips and for being absolutely convinced St. George took away his gorgeous plumage. (For the record, Vern never had feathers.) She also suggested the "man cold," but Vern ended up with flu instead. Because fever dreams in a dragon are hilarious.

Barbara Graves, who is writing a terrific vampire mystery (stay tuned!) had a couple of spot-on insights about Vern and Kitty. It only resulted in a couple of additional sentences but added another nuance to the relationship. Ann Lewis, who writes amazing Holmes pastiches as well as space opera, made astute points about the mystery that made it better.

Corinna Turner gave me some after-published feedback that made me rewrite the heaven scene. She pointed out that I seemed to advocate that Sister Grace's vows were being too easily dismissed by Vern's feelings of love. That was not my intention, but rather to make the choice between human and dragon more difficult. This edition has changes thanks to her honest feedback and willingness to fight for Sister Grace's honor.

A note of interest: Sometimes, in the DragonEye novels, you'll see Vern say, "I and so-and-so," rather than "So-and-so and I." Dragons come first. The exception is, of course, Sister Grace. Only once did he say, "Kitty and I," and it was when he was well and truly whammied. I think it haunts him sometimes.

You'll see HuVern again in *Live and Let Fly*. He keeps telling me scenes. Patience! More fun coming in the meantime.

About the Author

Does anyone read these? I don't always include a bio. I figure you bought this for Vern, not me, and he thinks that's right and proper.

As for me, I write about Vern, about nuns working in space, and about rednecks in a Star Trek-style universe. I occasionally write other things as the muse hits. One day, I want to try an actual romance. Siren Spell was too much fun. For my day job, I write business articles for Fit Small Business. (If more people bought Vern, I'd stop and write more books!)

I founded the Catholic Writers' Guild, and most of my friends hail from there. I recently started standup comedy lessons. They're a lot of fun, but I'm definitely funnier in story than on stage.

If you want to keep up with my adventures in person and on print, sign up for my newsletter at http://sendfox.com/fabianspace.

There's More Fun in FabianSpace!

DragonEye Series
Science Fiction

Space Traipse: Hold My Beer

The Old Man and the Void

Dex's Way

Discovery

The Rescue Sisters short stories

Fantasy

Mind Over Mind

Mind Over Psyche

Mind Over All

Hilarious Horror

Neeta Lyffe, Zombie Exterminator, in Zombie Death Extreme!

Neeta Lyffe in I Left My Brains in San Francisco

Neeta Lyffe in Shambling in a Winter Wonderland